Lily blinked, but it took her too long to process the piercing blue of his eyes.

The *familiarity* of those piercing blue eyes. She froze.

No. Her jaw dropped but no sound emerged. It wasn't possible. It was absolutely *not* possible that the man who'd traveled with her was—

A doppelganger. A look-alike. Anyone but *him*.

"Keep moving," he clipped roughly, dropping her arm to reposition his cap while she gaped in appalled astonishment.

His hair was uncharacteristically mussed because *she'd* twisted her fingers in it while he'd kissed up the inside of her thigh. And again while he'd *screwed* her into a brainless, blissful mess. *This* was such a mess.

"Come on. Do you want someone to see us?" His authoritative order shocked complete realization into her.

He clearly didn't want to be seen and definitely not with *her*. Because he wasn't some onboard courier who dealt with "paperwork." He was Massimo Hearnshawe, the squillionaire CEO of Hearnshawe Auto Group. There were layers and layers of management between them, but at the end of the day, this man was ultimately her *boss*.

USA TODAY bestselling author **Natalie Anderson** writes emotional contemporary romance full of sparkling banter, sizzling heat and uplifting endings—perfect for readers who love to escape with empowered heroines and arrogant alphas who are too sexy for their own good. When she's not writing, you'll find Natalie wrangling her four children, three cats, two goldfish and one dog...and snuggled in a heap on the sofa with her husband at the end of the day. Follow her at natalie-anderson.com.

Books by Natalie Anderson

Harlequin Presents

The Boss's Stolen Bride
My One-Night Heir

Innocent Royal Runaways

Impossible Heir for the King
Back to Claim His Crown

Billion-Dollar Bet

Billion-Dollar Dating Game

Convenient Wives Club

Their Altar Arrangement
Boss's Baby Acquisition
Greek Vows Revisited

Enemy Tycoons

Enemies Until After Hours

Visit the Author Profile page
at Harlequin.com for more titles.

BOSS'S MILE-HIGH BABY

NATALIE ANDERSON

Harlequin

PRESENTS

MIX
Paper | Supporting responsible forestry
FSC® C021394

Recycling programs for this product may not exist in your area.

ISBN-13: 978-1-335-21382-2

Boss's Mile-High Baby

Copyright © 2026 by Natalie Anderson

Harlequin Enterprises ULC
22 Adelaide St. West, 41st Floor
Toronto, Ontario M5H 4E3, Canada
www.Harlequin.com

HarperCollins Publishers
Macken House, 39/40 Mayor Street Upper,
Dublin 1, D01 C9W8, Ireland
www.HarperCollins.com

Printed in Lithuania

BOSS'S
MILE-HIGH BABY

For the gorgeous on the grid—Carlos, Charles, Alex and George—thanks for the inspiration!!!

CHAPTER ONE

'I DIDN'T THINK fans were allowed unaccompanied garage access.' Massimo Hearnshawe hit Pause and stared at the image, regrettably unable to freeze his instant rage with as much ease.

Andre, his highly paid race director, leaned over to see what Massimo was fixated on. 'Oh, she's not a fan. She works for us.'

'In what capacity?' Massimo questioned. He was too tired to deal with unnecessary drama and this was definitely drama.

The woman had her back to the camera so Massimo couldn't see her face, but he *could* see his young cousin's expression. Emiliano Costa, Massimo's talented, fast-as-fury driver, was serving a smile so charming it would slide the panties off any straight woman in a ninety-mile radius, and the interest lighting his eyes was unmistakable.

As the youngest driver to be promoted to P1 Global, the world's premier car-racing competition, the kid had more than enough to prove even before factoring in the added pressure of his family pedigree. He'd gained his P1 Global licence the day he'd turned eighteen last year and gone on to win rookie of the year despite barely being in the championship for enough of the races to be eligible. This was his first complete season and while he was performing well, a woman was *not* the distraction he needed.

'She's in Conrad's mechanic crew,' Andre replied.

Conrad was Hearnshawe's other driver—experienced, a proven race winner, married with two young children. Massimo had recruited him three years ago to mentor Emiliano and accumulate solid points while they got the car more competitive. The plan was progressing. Conrad was consistently making minor podium appearances, while Emiliano had come fourth in this afternoon's race here in Canada. They were *very* close.

It's not enough to be fast; you must be first.

Echoes of family expectation aggravated Massimo's exhaustion. He'd worked until the small hours for the three nights he'd been here, progressing deals within the broader company. He'd been finalising an auto group contract just now when the video had popped up. He stared harder at the screen. The mechanic's hair was tucked beneath a forest green *Hearnshawe Racing* cap, exposing her long neck and slender shoulders—her refined elegance at odds with the loose team polo swamping her frame. 'Then why is Emiliano talking to her?'

While their garages were side by side, while they were part of the same team, Emiliano had an entire crew of his own mechanics to talk to.

'I'm not sure,' Andre muttered.

Instant red flag.

Massimo was more than Emiliano's cousin and boss. He'd been his *guardian* for the past five years and there was nothing he wouldn't do to *protect* the kid. In this sport, elite athletes melded with exceptional engineering;

it was a seductive combination that attracted the world's most powerful, the most famous celebrities, the royals, the wealthy. And the wannabes. Sharks constantly circled. Sometimes those sharks were small and beautiful. There were temptations and traps on every turn *off* the track. But there was no way Massimo would allow anything to destroy Emiliano's racing career, and he knew how easily it happened. *Distraction* could destroy everything. It had destroyed Massimo's racing chances all those years ago.

His inattention hadn't just caused his own accident; he'd killed his parents.

He wasn't letting anything like that happen to his cousin. He eliminated any distraction Emiliano encountered. He'd done it before and he'd do it again now.

With twenty-three races through the season, the concentration and commitment required from a driver was immense. There was an exceptional burden of travel, physical training, competing, while the world clamoured for attention. Over the years, Massimo had engaged coaches, nutritionists, PTs, private tutors, doctors and sports psychologists to help Emiliano. He'd created a comprehensive team to provide a layer of protection, ensuring that the kid had the best possible professional help, because Massimo couldn't provide the personal. But even with all that in place, even with his innate drive and often declared intention to be the best ever, Emiliano had succumbed to the attentions of an older woman. She'd manipulated him, groomed him, until Massimo had managed to see it and step in. He'd unilaterally blocked her access and encouraged his cousin to focus on what he really wanted. Emiliano insisted that was driving, but the kid was now almost nineteen and as headstrong as he was talented, and to Massimo it was utterly obvious *why* he was so animatedly chatting to this particular mechanic.

She was stunning. He touched the screen and the short video replayed on the social media platform favoured by millions. It was impossible to hear what they were saying but Emiliano couldn't control his smile nor the flush in his cheeks. The comments piling in beneath the clip increased Massimo's concern. Rumour and conjecture were the last things his cousin needed and would be equally invasive for the mechanic. *She* possibly needed protection, too. But mostly Massimo didn't trust anyone who entered Emiliano's sphere. He vetted everyone.

'What do we know about her?' Massimo flexed his shoulders as he watched the clip loop over, his tension increasing with every replay.

Andre scrolled through his tablet before responding. 'Shane hired her a couple months ago. This was her first travelling weekend.'

Massimo frowned. Shane was Hearnshawe's number-one mechanic—salt of the earth, best in the entire pit lane and so highly regarded that other teams regularly tried to poach him. He would never recruit someone who wasn't supremely skilled at the job. But while Massimo respected Shane, he needed to see the woman's pedigree for himself.

'Show me her details.'

It took less than a minute for Massimo to skim the sparse text. Lily Jones was twenty-three, had basic mechanic qualifications but had built an impressive amount of experience in junior karting before levelling up through the categories. Furthermore, her references were excellent. Unfortunately, these facts didn't ease Massimo's tension; he was *more* worried. 'Where's Shane now?'

'Already on the way home.'

'And she's with him and the rest of the staff?'

Andre took back his tablet. With over a hundred employees travelling to each race, it was a massive logistical exercise and it took him a moment to scroll through the spreadsheet. 'No.'

'No? What are her travel arrangements?' Massimo felt a pressing need to know *exactly* where Lily Jones was this instant.

His cousin was meant to have dined with his trainer before retiring early at the hotel, but was something else going on?

'Uh…' Andre flicked through more screens. 'She's on the cargo flight. Takes off in an hour.'

'Cargo?' Startled, Massimo glanced up. For races beyond Europe, the cars and kit were sent through the night on chartered cargo flights. 'Why?'

'Sometimes we send a courier with new components. Maybe that's the situation here.'

Except this was the journey *home*, not the trip from the factory to the next race. Massimo watched the video once more, grimly noting the elegant arch of her neck and the tantalising glimpse of her fine-boned jaw as she laughed. A few strands of dark blond hair had escaped her cap and he absently wondered how long it was. He *shouldn't* wonder. But just like Emiliano in the video, Massimo couldn't stop staring, and the tiredness that had slowed his progress over the past hour now vanished. He was a details man. As CEO of Hearnshawe Auto Group, he had to be. There was an insane amount to manage.

Their main business had long been high-end luxury road cars, but twenty years ago their popularity had started to decline. Ten years ago, Massimo had snatched the reins and steered them in a different direction. The direction his father would have taken had he lived.

The elite motor-sport arm had always been a side project, but Massimo had poured resources into reviving it. Now it brought billions in sponsorship deals, merchandise and global brand awareness. Furthermore, his recent diversification into luxury products—for those living and loving the Hearnshawe lifestyle—was increasingly successful. The entire conglomerate was increasingly successful, but it had taken every ounce of Massimo's time to achieve it. In his mind, Hearnshawe's resurgence would only be complete when they had both P1 Global trophies—fastest driver, fastest car. Today's race had been the fifth in this year's series. Both Conrad and Emiliano had scored points, pushing Hearnshawe Racing into third place in the car-engineering competition. That was the best ranking they'd had in years, not yet first, but they were finally on the brink.

Massimo's temper lifted, firing fuel into his system. He would allow *nothing* to disrupt the trajectory of Hearnshawe's success. He would restore the honour, triumph, reputation—he lived only to fulfil that legacy. He wouldn't let Emiliano mess everything up by fooling around with an employee.

The responsibility for both of them ultimately rested with Massimo. *He* had to ensure Emiliano kept his focus; *he* had to ensure his employee's safety. So he needed to know more about Lily Jones—where she'd come from, what she really wanted from her work at Hearnshawe. He would ensure neither was a risk to the other.

Aside from sitting in the race car, there wasn't a job

within Hearnshawe that Massimo couldn't and wouldn't do himself. While he'd prefer to question Shane discreetly, the lead mechanic was already in the air and out of reach. Which meant Massimo had to learn all he needed to know about Lily Jones directly from her. He'd spent years suppressing his innate spontaneity, but this impulse was both imperative and undeniable.

'Get me on that flight,' he muttered.

Andre gaped at him. 'Sorry?'

'Get me on that cargo flight. *Now.*'

Lily Jones climbed the steep stairs onto the plane, relief seeping into her with every step. She could sit and sleep so very soon. She'd just survived the best, most exhausting, week of her life. Nailed her first away race as a mechanic for Conrad Tate, *Hearnshawe Racing's* number-one driver. Sure, she wasn't yet in the pit crew—clad in a helmet, working the wheel gun in the lightning-fast pit stops for both drivers—but she'd been on tyre prep and working on the car. Feedback had been minimal but she didn't need praise. She'd gone her entire life without it. She'd done her best and while she knew it was good, she aimed to get better still. To make that pit crew. This was the opportunity of a lifetime and she was doing nothing to screw it up. Head down, eyes on the job, no distractions. One week down. Seventeen to go.

Cargo flights were generally scheduled later than passenger jets and their journey times slightly slower, but in her limited experience the solitude and silence made it worth it. She wasn't bothered by the lack of windows, or that there were barely any amenities, no cabin crew offering snacks, no screens with on-board entertainment.

There was *space* from others. After almost a week of screeching rubber, of being around *thousands* of screaming spectators, she was more than ready for the lulling hum of the plane's engines. Yet, ironically, loneliness flickered. She wished she could share her experiences with someone who cared.

That wasn't going to be her family. They didn't consider P1 Global 'real' motorsport but rather a circus for spoilt posh playboys. They preferred a straight street drag race between cars illegally pimped up by themselves. They'd long derided her desire to work in elite motorsport even before they'd dismissed her from their lives completely. They weren't and would never be interested not only in P1 Global, but also in *her*. It shouldn't hurt anymore, but as she was only human, right now it still did.

You're just tired.

She could share her weekend stories with her mentor, Derek, and his wife, Jean, tomorrow. The old guy hadn't just helped her secure an apprenticeship; he and his wife had even provided accommodation when she'd been thrown out of her home. In fact, she was returning to the little caravan at the bottom of their property having given up her flat share because hopefully she'd be travelling so much with P1 Global. She'd have her performance review with Shane, the chief mechanic, next week and find out if she was now secure as away crew.

On board, she got to the small area for cargo couriers positioned behind the cockpit and crew sleeping area. There was a bank of just four seats. Two of them had containers strapped into them. The plane must be at max payload. She took the empty seat at the end, leaving the one next to her empty. Take-off was scheduled for just three minutes' time and she crossed her fingers no one else boarded. She could stretch out and sleep the entire time.

She glanced at her phone to check the time again. One minute to go and she was still alone. *Perfect.* Less perfect was the red flash of her phone battery icon, but it didn't matter; she intended to sleep the whole way. She glanced up at the sound of footsteps, hoping it was the pilots.

It wasn't.

Like her, he wore a cap but his wasn't emblazoned with a racing team logo; it was plain black and tugged so low it hid half his face. She glimpsed stubble on a chiselled jaw but honestly, it was enough just taking in his body. Black jeans clung to long legs. A grey T-shirt stretched across wide shoulders. Her fleeting disappointment at not being alone swiftly morphed into a flicker of sensual interest. He was tall and carried a fancy leather satchel that was incongruous against such casual clothing. Definitely an on-board courier. She knew a cargo flight held less risk of interference than a commercial passenger liner, and while it took a slower time in the air, there was a faster exit on the ground. Maybe this man was delivering documents too sensitive to be emailed. Or something so important it needed timely, secure transport. He definitely looked like he could do secure. Lily enjoyed a decent action flick and he totally had the look to take the lead. There was a lethality and anonymity about him—walls up as he walked in. With that lean, visibly fit frame, he was probably ex-Special Forces—all strength and speed and body easily used for intimidation. There were no visible honour tattoos but she thought she saw a scar running down his forearm before he turned towards the loadmaster who'd arrived behind him.

'Taking off shortly.' The loadmaster pulled her veering thoughts back on track. 'Buckle up and read the safety sheet.'

Lily dutifully scanned the document, trying to ignore the heat rising within her as the hot-bodied courier took the seat beside her and fastened his belt.

'Here's a couple blankets. You can see the coffee machine.' The loadmaster gave them one each. 'Sorry—'

'Thanks, we'll be fine,' the courier interrupted.

Confident and calm, quite posh. Ex-military for sure. Probably had flown the route a billion times.

The cabin lights dimmed for take-off, leaving only the coffee machine LED casting a faint blue light over them. Which was a relief because she was sure her heated reaction to him had reached her cheeks in an almighty flush. The engines fired and the plane hurtled down the runway before rising steeply into the air. As it levelled out, Lily toed off her trainers and spread the blanket on her lap. She would regulate her breathing—her reaction to him—and get some much needed sleep.

'Guessing from your cap that you went to the race this weekend,' he said.

Her flush flooded back at his huskiness and she was glad the cabin lights hadn't flicked back on.

'It's my job to,' she answered. 'I'm a mechanic for Hearnshawe Racing.'

It still thrilled her to say it.

'You mean with a socket and wrench?'

Lily felt her customary twin hits of pride and rebellion. Everyone always sounded surprised. She *liked* being a little unexpected, never wanted to be pigeonholed. So maybe she wasn't completely dissimilar to her law-breaking family.

'Is it so hard to believe?' she murmured.

'No, I just thought you were a courier. Why are you flying cargo? Isn't P1 Global all private jets and billion-dollar boats?'

'As well as super-fast cars?' She smiled in the darkness.

She'd assumed he'd be the strong, silent type but it seemed this gorgeously ripped guy wanted to talk to her with that low, husky voice for a while. Just the sound of him melted her cold, tired muscles.

'Not for the general employees,' she said.

Sometimes the teams chartered passenger planes to get crew to the farther-away races such as Sydney and Singapore, but mostly it was straight commercial. She honestly couldn't believe she might go to so many incredible countries. She never would have had the chance without this job.

'They don't treat you well?' Her ex-services hot courier asked. 'Is the prestige only for the main players?'

The glamour element of P1 Global was so far from Lily's realm of experience it was laughable. From the ridiculously good-looking drivers and their model girl-friends, to the musicians who pushed their agents to headline the post-race shows, to the celebrities visiting the pit and posing on the grid, even the *politicians*… That side of it was an elite, frankly alien, existence to hers.

Behind that scene it was hard work. Everyone on the team pushed to achieve. Only the finest of margins separated the top teams. Hundredths, even thousandths, of a second could make the difference between champagne celebrations or no points at all. And points meant money, development, speed. She adored the hard work and the lifestyle—the circus-like travel requirement, the prospect of being away for almost half the weeks in the year, was perfect for her.

'I'm treated amazingly well,' she replied. 'It's long hours but I have the chance to work on the fastest car in the world. P1 Global is the pinnacle of any mechanic's career.'

She felt rather than saw him nod.

'But you don't fly with the team?'

'Not this time.' She'd requested her own arrangements and had a contact in the cargo world. She'd just had to let the team director know the details. She liked the darkness and the peace and not being squished in with a couple hundred other people. But she couldn't resist engaging with her fellow passenger. 'I'm guessing you don't follow P1?'

'Well, it's just fast traffic going in circles, right?' he mocked lightly. 'Rich guys in their flash toys that they can't even take on the road.'

He sounded like her brothers. She'd had this argument many times with them. 'Yeah,' she sighed playfully. '*Lots* of men with *lots* of money.'

'So *that's* the real attraction?' he drawled.

Points off for being patronising. 'No, the real attraction is the smell of burning rubber and the sound of screeching tires fighting for grip.'

'Seriously?'

'Fully,' she said firmly. 'It's *so* good. It's hot and loud and fast. *Every* sense struggles to keep up with the input—sight, sound, smell. If you blink you miss them fly past. It's pure adrenaline. The technology is mind-blowing. Then there are the fans—the roar of that crowd is insane. Go to a race weekend, then you'll understand.'

'So you've always been into it?'

'I was basically born in a garage. Cars are the family business.'

'In P1 Global?'

'No.' She was hardly legacy elite like the billionaire family team she worked for. 'Just a small local garage.' She fudged the truth.

'They must be incredibly proud of you.'

She sighed. A normal, nice, loving family might be proud, but her family was neither normal nor loving. 'Unfortunately, you can't always please family.'

'No matter what you do?' he added lightly. 'Yeah, I hear you.'

Because he'd experienced the same?

'Sucks, doesn't it?' she murmured. 'Can't change them, though.'

'No. Definitely can't.'

She didn't want to think about her family let alone talk about them. Like Hearnshawe Racing they worked on cars that weren't road legal—modifying them to be faster than their intended capability. Street racing had been the start; getaway cars the later purpose.

'Does the team use you as their poster girl?' the courier asked. 'I'm assuming you're one of the few female mechanics they have.'

'I'm not the first and I'm definitely not going to be the last. Definitely not on any posters. The number-one mechanic wouldn't stand for it.'

The cliché of being a hot chick on the shop floor wasn't

her. For one thing, she wasn't hot and in Lily's view just surviving—let alone *excelling*—as one of the few women in any male-dominated world required one of two options. She could either embrace and accentuate her feminine differences, or she could hide them. She opted for the latter. Hiding who she was was her go-to. She'd been overlooked and underestimated her entire life, but now she used it as an invisibility cloak she pulled on at will. She always wore her team cap tugged low and the collar of her team polo shirt turned up to expose as little of her pale skin as possible. She couldn't hide her stature—high heels weren't exactly a thing on a garage floor—so she was undeniably petite, but she was strong. She needed not to be as good as the guys, but *better*—just to hold her own. Which meant that being alone and away from the scene—well, almost alone—for a few hours now was an immense relief. With no pressure to perform she could completely relax. Given this guy didn't even like P1 Global, she was safe.

'So you're a courier,' she said idly. 'Documents?'

'Paperwork keeps me pretty busy.' He didn't expand further.

Yeah, he was definitely in security. He probably had highly sensitive, eyes-only, no-digital-footprint papers in that bag.

Lily relaxed more, ready for some rest except her stomach rumbled loud enough to be heard over the engine hum. *Damn.*

'Didn't you have dinner before boarding?' he teased.

She hadn't had the time. She'd been crazy busy with the pack-out then too tired to be bothered grabbing something on her way to the airport. She should have.

'There's only coffee on board,' he said. 'And you can't

steal the crew dinner. Wouldn't want to risk our safety with a hangry pilot.'

Yeah, he'd definitely done this before.

'Fortunately…' He reached into that satchel and pulled out a packet that he opened then shook it towards her. 'Please don't refuse politely. I assure you they're nice. I'm happy to share mostly because I don't want to listen to your stomach for the next seven hours.'

'Fair point.' She chuckled. 'Thank you.' Chocolate-covered almonds. Next-level delicious and Lily was ravenous. 'These are really good.'

'Don't hold back,' he teased as she reached for more.

'Don't offer if you don't mean it.'

Wordlessly, he handed her the rest of the bag, but then still kept eating them as well. They both chuckled, then snacked in companionable silence. Lily watched the LED on the coffee machine flicker with ominous inconsistency, not that she wanted coffee, she was desperate for sleep, but it was about the only glow in the place and being in complete darkness might be a bit much.

'They were just what I needed, thanks,' she murmured when they finished the pack and he put the wrapper away.

'My pleasure.'

He was just being polite. She was just overreacting—reading intimacy into everything because she'd been without for so long. She removed her cap, uncoiled her hair and lightly massaged her scalp to chill herself out. She'd sleep soon. Hopefully. Once she finally grew accustomed to sitting next to the hot courier—except her awareness of him was only worsening.

'Your hair is so long. How do you fit it under the cap?'

In that too-tight bun she'd just undone. 'It needs a trim but I never have time to get to the hairdresser.'

'Good,' he muttered bluntly. 'You shouldn't cut it.'

His audible appreciation made her flush all over again, but to her disappointment, he didn't take his cap off. He just tugged it lower over his eyes and sank into the seat. Lily's disappointment deepened.

'So you're not interested in the drivers at all?' he asked after a moment. 'Not for their money, of course, but they've got skills, right?'

'Oh please. They're not my type.'

She liked Conrad well enough. He was a decent family guy. But she kept away from Emiliano—young, connected to the Hearnshawe family, he lived a far too public life for her liking. But he'd asked her about tyre compound earlier today and had been interesting. She didn't want to garner attention. She just wanted to get on with her job, and eventually truly excel.

'No?' The courier sounded typically sceptical.

Lily rolled her eyes even though he couldn't see her. 'They're extremely arrogant—I get they need bulletproof confidence given they're putting their lives on the line, but it can be a bit much. And the risk itself—I don't know how their family even watch the races. They have an insane schedule that leaves little room for fun—it's all diet and exercise plans. They have millions of fans sliding into their DMs, chasing them for photos every time they step outside. I can't think of anything worse than trying to compete with the models, dancers and singers or the minor royalty who want to be seen with them. No, thank you.'

'Wow. You've given this some serious thought,' he teased.

'About what kind of relationship I might want eventually, sure. The reality is that any elite athlete, any highly successful person, makes sacrifices to get where they are. They have to be driven, with singular focus for years. *Nothing* is more important to them than that goal. Definitely not a girlfriend.'

'You want to be first?'

Yes, it would be very nice to be placed first. Just once. Just for someone. 'Give me someone ordinary. Someone average. With a heart that can be wholly mine.'

She paused, embarrassed. She'd just revealed too much personal truth. She couldn't think how to lighten it again.

'Still,' he mused flippantly. 'They're good-looking.'

She chuckled, relieved. 'You want an introduction?'

'You offering?'

'Never gonna happen.'

'Because you want to keep me for yourself?'

'You're as arrogant as they are,' she mocked.

'Ouch.' His shoulders shook.

But she just knew his confidence was innate—he had surety in his unbranded clothes and own skin—no super speed or stratospheric success necessary.

'Then why not take me there?' he asked.

'Because I want to keep my job,' she said firmly. 'I've worked too hard to get to where I am to screw it up by bringing random people into the garage. Plus, I wouldn't do it to the guys.'

'You're loyal.'

Damn right she was. Despite what her family thought.

'I'm merely one small cog in a very large team machine, but if we each do our thing, we get results.'

'Good for you,' he murmured.

She softened, stupidly pleased at his support and too tired to stay sensible. She couldn't even see his face clearly yet her body was acting as if he was the hottest man on the planet. Just his voice had her melting and while she would never let the personal get in the way of work, that wasn't to say she wouldn't play with someone *outside* of the racing world…

'I bet guys hit on you all the time,' he muttered. Apparently, his thoughts were tracking along a similar line. 'You're their fantasy come to life.'

There seriously weren't many but it was flattering that he seemed to think it. It had been forever since she'd experienced anything remotely intimate. Five years ago her boyfriend had taken her brother's side and she'd been utterly alone since.

'They just want free merch,' she said, trying not to notice the length of his thigh pressing against hers. 'I've been hit with the worst pickup lines.'

'P1 puns?' He suddenly laughed.

It was an irresistibly sexy laugh. Lily couldn't help laughing with him. 'Like you wouldn't believe.'

'Try me.'

'Oh, they want to warm me up, rev my engine, explore my curves with their long, straight…'

'Wow,' he drawled. 'I bet they assume you like it *fast* or that you prefer hard over soft—'

'Without checking whether I'm slick—'

'Because they just want to kiss your kerb or brush your walls?'

'Diabolically *dreadful*.' She giggled. 'And you're holding out. *You* know some racing jargon. I'm thinking you're a closet fan.'

He stiffened slightly. 'Well, I do own a car…'

'*That's* the mistake,' Lily murmured playfully, enjoying the tragic jokes. 'Guys assume *I'm* the car. But I'm not. Nor am I the tyres.'

'You're the driver.'

'*Exactly.*' She rode out the ridiculous analogy. 'Maybe I like the challenge of a hard-to-control machine. One with an engine powerful enough to get me sixty times around the circuit as *fast* as possible.'

'So you do like it fast,' he noted. 'You want to hit the apex?'

'Sure, but to do that I need full power and pace.' She rolled with it. 'Some downforce. All too often there's not enough grip and they burn through the rubber before the finish line.'

'Sounds like you need a better make and model. What if he's too powerful for you to control?'

Yeah, he was arrogant. And a rogue.

'Oh, I'm an *exceptional* driver,' she purred.

'Exceptional?' he echoed softly. 'You realise you've just taken the route straight to my heart.'

'Sorry, but I'm way too fast for you to handle. You can't catch me. Can't match my pace.'

'Maybe you should be careful. If you lose control you might crash and burn.'

'But I don't lose control,' she replied. 'I always hit the racing line.'

His laughter then was full-throttle amusement and fully attractive. Smiling wide, Lily slumped lower in her seat, wholly relaxing at last. It was a simple joy to share weak jokes with a handsome stranger who smelt good and sounded better. She watched the coffee machine's LED display flicker haphazardly before finally failing for good and plunging them into darkness.

'Oh look at that.' She shook her head and then muttered the commentator's catch phrase for the start of every race. 'It's lights out and away we go.'

CHAPTER TWO

MASSIMO WISHED HE really could put the pedal to the metal and floor it somewhere with her. The bad racing banter had gotten worse and worse but he'd relished every silly pun and he didn't want it to stop now. Which it would—instantly—if she knew who he really was. The lack of light saved him. Bought him more time. More intimacy.

He'd *almost* admitted it but she'd assumed he was a courier and he'd not corrected her. He'd not *lied*. But he felt uncomfortable. Except if he confessed all now, she would be furious; she'd want to know why and how and they were both too tired to deal with that discussion. He'd tell her nearer the end of the flight. Yeah, he was a selfish jerk, but there was no point in making the next few hours a complete awkward misery.

'It doesn't seem as if that light's going to come back on,' she murmured. 'This really is a poor girl's private plane.'

'A what?'

'My team teased me with that when I told them I was flying cargo, but I think it's great.'

It was extremely different to Massimo's private jet. He had a decent sofa on there on which they could stretch out together and sleep. Or not sleep. They could—

What the hell? He mentally berated himself. The woman wanted peace and solitude, not a leering jerk invading her personal space.

'I'll tell you a secret,' she whispered, before yawning.

He leaned closer, eager to hear anything she wanted to share, especially something secret. 'What?'

'Canada was my first full race weekend with the team.' She spoke soft and slow, sounding disappointingly sleepy. 'I'm not the wheel gun-blazing super-pit-crew queen I made myself out to be.'

Yeah, but he understood the need for some bravado, a veneer of quiet confidence to hold her own. P1 Global was a tough enough nut to crack without the additional gender imbalance she faced. 'Well, maybe not *yet*, but I'm sure it won't be long before you are.' He meant every word. She was a true enthusiast, living her dream life with the job she'd long wanted. 'Was it everything you'd hoped it?'

'And then some.' She yawned again. 'It was amazing.'

He sat in the darkness, enjoying the satisfaction in her voice. Not wanting to ruin her moment, or for the moment to end, he played ignorant and couldn't resist asking. 'Where's the next race?'

He waited for her to answer. But there was silence.

'Lily?' He winced, realising he'd used her name when he shouldn't know it.

But despite that mistake, she still didn't answer. He leaned close enough to see her face and saw she'd fallen asleep. Just like that.

He sat back, oddly miffed. Women didn't fall asleep in his presence. They flicked their hair. They flirted. They scrambled to grasp and hold his attention. And yes, he was spoilt because of it. He was also jaded and untrusting. He avoided social media like the plague. Avoided *anything* social like the plague, knowing people wanted anything and everything from him—but not *actually* him. He only attended work events with elite-level sponsors now—so spending twenty minutes *not* being sucked up to, not flattered or basically frisked for money, but being treated as an ordinary guy was weird. It hadn't happened since he was eight years old and finally pulled into the Hearnshawe family fold.

Her manner towards him would change once she knew. *Everyone* changed when they realised who he was. It was unbelievably nice to be anonymous for a few minutes. He wanted more of the light banter and laughter. He wanted more of her secrets. He wanted more of her palpable excitement and joy when talking about being at a race weekend. He fully felt the same thrill.

She wasn't a threat to Emiliano. She'd been adamant about her disinterest in any drivers—certainly not one four years younger than her and still a teenager. She'd had the driver faults nailed. They were all arrogant, egotistical, single-minded. They had to be. But *she* was driven, too. Making it as a mechanic to P1 Global was a serious achievement. She'd meant it when she'd said she'd worked too hard to mess it up. Which made him inclined to believe her about everything, including the part about wanting to be placed *first*.

That wasn't something he could ever offer anyone. For him, the company would *always* come first. He owed that to his father.

But Lily was engaging and gorgeous and no wonder his cousin had been hanging on her every word earlier today. He'd been an overly suspicious idiot, but he'd fix it. He'd confess—to a degree—and step back. Though he would insist Emiliano be kept away from her; the kid needed to concentrate. He'd filter the instruction via Shane rather than antagonising his cousin directly. He breathed out the niggle of guilt and settled lower into his seat. He might as well rest now. Except her scent enveloped him; her words and passion lingered in his mind. Refreshing. Bewitching. Beautiful. Maybe no threat to Emiliano, but a terrible temptation to him.

No. He didn't get tempted. He wouldn't let that happen. He would tell her who he was the second they woke.

Heaviness gradually invaded his limbs. He felt an overwhelming sense of peace and well-being descend like a warm weight upon him. He blinked drowsily and realised there was an *actual* weight. She'd slumped sideways, her head pressed against his biceps. The armrest between them was digging into his ribs; it had to be doing the same to hers. He roused himself enough to carefully push her upright. She didn't stir as he slowly lifted the armrest, making their seat a double. She still didn't rouse. He was ruefully reminded of how unaware she was of him. He could just make out her features—her turned-up nose, the full pout of her lips, her delicate, high cheekbones. She was even prettier than he'd imagined from that video clip. Only now, to his infinite regret, she didn't slump back towards him.

The banked-up tiredness from the past few weeks hit full force. He couldn't remember why he'd even boarded this damned plane anymore. All he knew was that it was dark and warm and he was wrapped in her lightly fragrant scent. He shifted and she tumbled close again. He froze for a moment, then gently wrapped his arm around her shoulder, keeping his hand above the small blanket. Not copping a feel but getting them both comfortable. He carefully stretched out, closed his eyes again and let her softness melt his muscles—determined to suppress the desire stirring low in his body. He would sleep so very soon. In this last second, he would enjoy these few moments of innocent intimacy with a stranger. He would forget who she was. Who *he* was. In the dark, with the low hum of the engines lulling them, nothing mattered anymore. Drowsily, almost unconscious, he pulled her closer, absurdly comfortable despite the bare-bones surroundings. And for the first time in forever, he fully relaxed.

Lily woke with a feeling of supreme comfort, realising she was pressed against solid, breathing security. Her hand was splayed on his abs and her breathing was in sync with the gentle rise and fall of his chest beneath her cheek. She would die of mortification at being all over him like a vine if it weren't for the fact that both his arms were wound around her—one heavy across her shoulder, the other stretched over her waist and resting on her hip. Holding her close. *Safe.* Thus cocooned, Lily was warmed through to the bone, every muscle within her lax. The humming plane engine provided a sound screen, adding an additional layer of privacy to the velvety dark, sensual sanctuary already enshrouding them. She had no idea what time it was nor how long they had left in the air, and she couldn't remember the last time she'd been held like this. Tenderly. Intimately. *Fiercely.*

Honestly, it had been years since she'd been held at all. More than five since her brother had gone, since her boyfriend had broken up with her, since her parents had thrown her out of her home. She'd not allowed anyone this close since. She'd made it a rule never to get involved with anyone remotely related to work, but as she only had time for work, she only met men from work and therefore, they were *all* excluded. But this guy had nothing to do with her job. He was nothing but a fellow traveller, passing through her life for a few hours. And as rusty as she was, as vaguely experienced, she knew their chemistry had been instant and intense. In the glimpse she'd had of his body, in his husky voiced, easy-going interest and dry amusement, there had been awareness. They'd shared little really, yet it was more than enough for a deep resonance to strike within. The vibrations between them still hummed. He was a decent guy—supportive. She never shared her dreams but he'd unquestioningly believed she'd make it to wheel-gun queen, and now she couldn't resist the temptation to press that touch closer to his perfection, breathing in his musky scent. She didn't want him to wake. She wanted to stay like this forever— *craved* this precious closeness. So she breathed it in. She was so engrossed in appreciating the sensations, that she didn't notice the subtle quickening of the rise and fall beneath her at first. She gently spread her fingers, feeling more of his broad but lean chest, stilling as she grazed the steely point of his nipple with her thumb. Heat filled her and she couldn't resist swiping her thumb across it again. His sharp inhalation filled the tiny space between them. His heavy, all-encompassing arms tightened.

'I'm so sorry,' she whispered, mortified. 'I fell asleep on you.'

She went to pull away but his arms tightened more. She froze. There was a breathless beat before he suddenly relaxed his hold but she didn't straighten and move away from him as she should.

'Don't apologise,' he murmured. 'I liked it.'

'Yeah?'

'Yeah.' He sounded sleepy but his arms flexed again. Keeping her right where she ached to be. *Close.*

'Me, too.'

Wary, yet unable to resist tiptoeing towards some wonderful, fragile temptation, Lily slowly slid her palm farther up his chest. She heard another hitch in his breath but he said nothing. He didn't stop her. Emboldened by the warmth and the darkness, by the leashed power in his firm hold, she gently explored more—skimming her hand up to the neck of his tee and across to the bare warm skin of his throat. He seemed to stop breathing entirely as Lily fluttered her fingertips all the way up to his jaw. It was roughened by stubble, but still sharp; he was all masculine angles. She grazed her fingertip—the lightest brush, an illicit, irresistible touch—across his lower lip and felt the welcoming swipe of his tongue. Adrenaline surged as anticipation flooded her.

Green light.

It took nothing to raise her head and lightly brush her lips over his. His arms instantly tightened. He *had* been holding back on his power. His lips parted and met hers. She gasped as he groaned, lost in drowsy, erotic appreciation. He cupped her face and deepened the kiss, taking control, but she kissed him harder—matching his ardour. She didn't want to speak. Didn't want him to, either. She didn't want anything to stop this moment. She needed nothing but this because she'd never been kissed like this in her life.

Yet, all too soon, kisses weren't enough. She wasn't close enough. She unfastened her seat belt and he immediately pulled her onto his lap and wound his arms tight around her, not breaking the seal of their mouths. Ignited, she kissed him harder, increasingly hot and aching. He combed his fingers through her hair, toying with the silky length before settling his heavy palm on the nape of her neck, keeping his kisses lush and deep. He shifted beneath her and she succumbed to the carnal urge to climb right on him. She tore her lips free, snatching a breath, and managed to straddle one of his thighs. He kissed down the side of her neck, gently tracing over her collarbones, setting off trails of pure fire that arrowed low. She clamped her thighs harder around his as he skimmed his hand beneath her tee and lifted it up and off her. It was hot, fast, unstoppable. He teased his thumbs over her bra and flexed that thigh beneath her, encouraging her to ride. With exquisite, torturous strokes he guided her pace. The delicious friction of the rock-hard muscle right beneath her core felt incredible—igniting her. She knew it took both discipline and genetic blessing to have a body like his. She groaned, wishing she could get him naked, get closer still. Apparently, he read her mind. She moaned as he unfastened her jeans and slid his hand into her pants, but her position blocked wholly intimate access. It didn't matter. He got one finger right where she needed it, applied the exact pressure she ached for. Quivering, she rocked and he rubbed and it was unbearably hot and slick and hungry.

'Go on, gorgeous,' he growled against her breasts. 'Get it.'

She needed no encouragement; she was almost there.

He sucked her nipple deep into his mouth, bra and all—*hard*. She bucked, barely biting back her scream as pleasure smashed through her in ecstatic, intense waves, over and over until she slumped against him, breathless and sweltering and unable to believe she'd hit that high, that hard, that quick.

Now he roved his hands carefully over her back as the spasms slowly ebbed. His was the lightest, most tender touch, but she didn't want careful; she wanted complete.

'Don't hit the brakes too soon,' she muttered unevenly.

His huff of amusement warmed her, but he tensed more—which ought to have been impossible.

'Then you need to pick the braking point,' he growled.

Oh there wasn't going to be a braking point.

'You do realise that was just the qualifying lap,' she murmured. 'We're not stopping until we both get the chequered flag.'

The bad race jargon banter was perfectly unserious, but the underlying meaning was so important. She *desperately* didn't want him to stop.

'I'm willing to race.' He slid his hands down the outside of her thighs. 'But you're the one in pole position. You set the pace.'

Fine by her. *So* fine. She tugged his tee up and off the same way he'd discarded hers. His body was pure ripped fire. She kissed across his chest, nuzzling closer, and unclasped his belt. He worked on his jeans and she shifted to straddle both his legs and bring her core flush to his. She moaned as she finally felt his rigid arousal right where she wanted it most.

He spread both hands beneath her butt. 'Time to push.'

'Go full throttle? I dare you to unleash all your power.'

She felt him coil and he suddenly rose, lifting her with him in a fierce movement. He took two steps and pressed her against the wall, grinding close. She gasped, delight-stunned and desperate for more. She wriggled to help her jeans slide down, finally shaking one leg completely free and immediately hooked it around his slim hips. His rough groan was her undoing. Desire unfurled—unravelling every thought, destroying all caution. He was nitrous oxide turbo-charging her engine, but where she'd taken the lead before, he now overtook—gaining control of track position and pace. He pressed close, his hands swift and skilled, scorching every inch of her skin. She'd never felt as wanted in her life and had never wanted a man to claim her so intensely. She'd not even seen his face properly but it didn't matter. She felt him now—kissing his high cheekbones, tracing his straight nose and the stubble on his lean, sharp jaw. She ran her hand down his warm neck and nuzzled closer. Needing more. 'Please—'

'Safety car,' he breathed hard, then groaned. 'Need to slow the pace.'

'Why?' she wailed.

'Unsafe conditions.' He panted. 'Helmet. Flame protection. Can't let the celebrations make things messy.'

It was an appalling muddle of racing metaphors but she finally got what he meant and she froze, devastated. 'I don't have—'

'Give me a second.' He stepped away, rummaging in his satchel in the dark.

Did the guy have condoms in his courier bag? Lily blinked. Oh well, good for him and lucky for her. Maybe those few minutes breathing space should've given her a chance to see sense—to be a little cautious about having sex with a stranger. Instead, they had the opposite effect. This had been the best weekend ever and she was ending it with a bang. She was so *here* for this with him and he definitely knew what he was doing. She heard his muttered oath of relief and very nearly cried with joy herself. A moment later he was back before her. On his knees. She heard the rip of foil. Another muttered imprecation. She laughed—then gasped at the sudden slide of his hot mouth up the inside of her thigh. He pulled her panties off then gripped her hips, holding her still enough to taste her. She drove her fingers though his hair—desperate to let him plunder but needing so much more at the same time.

'I'm ready, I'm ready, I'm ready.' She pushed her hips forward in an unashamedly needy erotic invitation. 'Please. Please.'

With a muffled growl he suddenly stood. 'You want me to box?'

'Immediately.'

He grasped her waist hard and lifted her. She hooked both legs around his hips, moaning at the smooth, ravenous drag of his lips up her neck as he pinned her between him and the wall. For once, she loved her petite stature because being at his mercy like this was pure heaven.

'Don't lose grip,' he murmured.

'I won't.'

She caressed his steely body, savouring the flinch and flex of straining muscle. She palmed up his chest to his shoulders, curling her hands over them to hang on. As he lifted her an inch higher against the wall, she braced. For a moment their hot breath mingled, then their bodies collided. Hard.

'Oh!' she gasped, her muscles becoming like a vise as he surged into her.

He tensed and she muttered helplessly, 'It's been so long.'

'Same,' he whispered, shuddering as she gripped him. 'Feels good.'

'Yes.'

She sank into his kiss for only seconds before tearing her mouth free to sigh as he filled her. His possession was total, his pace fast, pushing closer and harder and giving her everything, utterly *everything* she wanted with rough rolls of his entire body. Electricity arced, energising them both as they became a slick, hot mass of locked limbs and desperate drive pulsing in the secret, dark heat.

She didn't care about anything else but this—would burn all the fuel in the world to find more of this pleasure with him. Everything escalated—*accelerated*—she stifled her screams against his shoulder as he unleashed on her, his hips pumping, pulling her into his fiery passion until she seized in a final moment of suspension before falling apart completely. With a final thrust, he muffled his raw growl against her neck and finished a hundredth of a second after her.

Lily kept her arms and legs locked around him as best she could given their trembling; kept her face buried in his shoulder. Flickers of unbearable ecstasy rippled relentlessly through every cell but slowly she became aware of gentle strokes—slow hands soothing her oversensitive skin; soft kisses silencing jangling nerves.

It was the most tender cool-down lap of her life and suddenly she wanted—

'Buckle up. We're landing in five.' The voice burst through the intercom with a loud crackle.

Shock snuffed Lily's hazy, heated bliss and the yearning resurging within her. He quickly—carefully—lowered her to her feet and they stumbled apart. Mortified, Lily untangled her jeans, desperately searched out her panties and squashed them into her pocket and shoved her feet back into her trainers. She fell back into her seat and fastened the lap belt, beyond grateful for the lack of light. Tension-filled stillness smashed that warm dream world. She didn't know what to say, so she was silent. He was quiet, too.

The noise of the descent and landing prevented conversation anyway. Or that was what she told herself. Honestly, she was still trying to process what had just happened. That searingly intimate moment had been so quick, so intense. So *perfect*. The problem was she already was yearning for a repeat, only his current vibe suggested this was definitely a one and done. Her first such event. Casual hook-ups might be common for him, but she was a complete novice. She tried to gather her scattered wits. Sure, they'd shared banter and chemistry. Sure, he'd given her the most amazing sexual experience of her life, but it only felt this soul-shatteringly important *because* she'd not had that many such experiences, right? Because she'd been lonely after a massive week.

As the plane taxied to the terminal, the lights flickered on. She was determined to keep her dignity. Definitely not make a fool of herself by asking him on a date. Given he'd put his cap back on and was angled away from her, she already knew what the answer would be.

So she would make a quick escape now. But the second the plane stopped he was out of his seat, his satchel slung over his shoulder. He clearly wanted a quick exit, too. Only he then picked up *her* duffel bag.

'I can manage it,' Lily said.

'I know.' He'd tugged his cap low again and didn't let go of her bag. She followed him down to the door. He tilted his head to one side, then the other, stretching the sides of his neck.

'That shouldn't have happened,' he muttered.

Lily dropped her gaze, stupidly hurt that he regretted it. He cleared his throat. 'I'm so—'

'Don't apologise,' she interrupted swiftly. She'd liked it. *Too much.*

'But—'

'Please.' She slammed her cap on her head. It was perfect to avoid looking into his eyes. She stepped forward to disembark ahead of him. 'It's no big deal.'

But she was stung. That had been the most amazing—admittedly insane, but most amazing—moment of her life. *Sex* life, not *entire* life. And at the time she'd been pretty sure he'd been into it so his backpedalling now was both mortifying and annoying. She heard him draw breath but swiftly moved the second the door opened. She didn't want to listen—didn't want this to be made *worse*.

There was no air bridge, just a steep staircase down to the tarmac and a painted line leading to the terminal. The grey drizzle dampened her already deflated mood.

'But—'

'Just forget about it.' She hurried to the bottom of the stairs.

'Forget?' Right behind her, his low voice turned harsh. 'How the *hell* am I ever going to forget that?'

CHAPTER THREE

STARTLED BY HIS raw admission—*gratified*—Lily almost slipped on the tarmac.

'Careful.' His hand clamped just above her elbow and he steadied her with a too-firm grip.

She was so flustered she could melt marshmallows on her flaming cheeks. Because she was hardly about to forget it, either. She risked a glance up, confused by the leashed lethality of both his tone and touch and the underlying need that remained in each. The dull light hit his stubbled face. Lily blinked but it took her too long to process the piercing blue of his eyes. The *familiarity* of those piercing cornflower-blue eyes. She froze. Right in the middle of the tarmac.

No. Her jaw dropped but no sound emerged. It wasn't possible. It was absolutely *not* possible that the man who'd travelled with her was—

A doppelganger. A lookalike. Anyone but *him*.

'Keep moving,' he clipped roughly, dropping her arm to reposition his cap while she gaped in appalled astonishment.

His hair was uncharacteristically mussed because *she'd* twisted her fingers in it while he'd kissed up the inside of her thigh. And again while he'd *screwed* her into a brainless, blissful mess. *This* was such a mess.

'Come on. Do you want someone to see us?' His authoritative order shocked complete realisation into her.

He clearly didn't want to be seen and definitely not with *her*. Because he wasn't some on-board courier who dealt with *paperwork*. He was Massimo Hearnshawe, the squillionaire CEO of Hearnshawe Auto Group. He was the man in charge of not just the elite motor racing team, but the enormous luxury car manufacturing company plus all the other add-on businesses within the massive conglomerate. There were layers and layers of management between them, but at the end of the day, this man was ultimately her *boss*. He owned everything. He had more money in his personal bank account than several small countries combined. As a result, he was the most eligible bachelor connected to P1 Global—in pretty much the world, actually. And that was before factoring in his stunning looks. He had more than that blessed body; he had the face of a freaking angelic aftershave model. She'd *felt* the angularity and symmetry of that chiselled jaw. Now she saw it in the early-morning light and yeah, cue the heavenly choirs.

But she also knew while Massimo Hearnshawe looked hot, he was actually ice-cold. Ruthlessly ambitious, legend had it he'd changed the locks on his own grandfather. The poor old guy had been out at his birthday lunch and come back to find he couldn't get into the company headquarters he'd presided over for forty-three years. Massimo had taken over *everything*. But since he'd been in charge, the company had thrived and the racing arm had become competitive again for the first time in decades.

She knew the man was famously private, allowing the public only the smallest glimpse into his rarefied world. He was barely seen in the garage on race weekends, preferring to watch from the privacy of his corporate suite—safely beyond the reach of the great unwashed and overly sycophantic. He was racing royalty—and driver Emiliano Costa's cousin. No wonder he'd been able to go along with all that stupid motoring innuendo. And this was absolutely the worst thing that could possibly have happened.

'Seriously, Lily. Let's go.'

That order shocked her into stillness all over again. 'How do you know my name?'

Because she'd never told him who she was, not in the entire time they were on that plane. He'd certainly never mentioned his, either.

He actually winced. 'We'll talk inside.'

'No.' She stayed still on the tarmac. 'You owe me an immediate explanation.'

'I'll give you that. *Inside*,' he repeated tightly.

She locked her muscles, refusing to fall in line, but as she glared at him, the pilots passed behind them with a deliberately wide swerve. She glanced to the side and saw the ground crew watching—*waiting*—to unload the plane. She turned and moved forward, furious at having to concede. She would get her answers the second they were alone.

But the brief wait for customs processing gave her enough breathing space to realise she didn't actually *want* a conversation. There was nothing that could be said to fix this. It was simply catastrophic.

He'd not told her who he was. But she'd not told him things, too.

Massimo might basically be aristocracy, but Lily came from a wannabe criminal dynasty. Where he was notoriously private, her family was small-time notorious. No one at P1 Global knew because Jones was a blessedly common name. She hid in plain sight—kept her head down and let her work speak for her—not only because she was one of the few females on the garage floor, but also because she didn't want anyone to become too curious about her or her background. She'd been so focused for so long and she'd worked too hard to allow anything to threaten her work ethic or her reputation, because her career was literally all she had left.

But what had just happened on that plane threatened her actual *job*. She had to fight for it. Somehow, she needed to shut this down and somehow, she needed to swerve past the intense disappointment that while it would be impossible to *forget*, it could *never* happen again. She was completely unsuitable for him to be connected to.

But Massimo Hearnshawe still had her duffel bag and he didn't relinquish it.

The customs officer smiled at them as if they were a couple. 'Nothing to declare?'

Speechless, she shook her head.

Massimo had barely answered before the customs officer waved them through and she strode towards the exit. He could keep her bloody bag. She probably wasn't going to need her team uniform anymore anyway—he wouldn't want her to work for his team now. Questions flooded her mind. Why was he even on that plane? How did he know who she was? What had he really wanted? Would he offer to pay her off now?

Her father would advise her to extract every penny she

could, but he was callous enough to get whatever he could from whomever he could and didn't give a damn about the damage he left behind. He certainly didn't give a damn about Lily. She'd been cut off when she'd not complied with his *family orders*. Maybe that was the only answer to this situation as well—complete distance.

'I'll give you a lift.'

Lily's rage mounted as Massimo had the temerity to put her bag into the car waiting for him before she'd even agreed. Because he was *that* accustomed to getting everything he wanted. 'No, thank you.'

'Get in the car.'

'Absolutely not, and you cannot force me to.' She bitterly smiled at the prospect of him trying to manhandle her into it. 'Do you know I actually thought you were ex-Special Forces?'

'You thought *what*?' A quizzical expression lit his face.

'I thought you were some kind of high-security courier.'

'Why on earth would you think that?'

'Because you're built like one.' She waved a hand at his towering physique. 'Tough and lean and you didn't have baggage. I thought there was important paperwork in the fancy leather satchel.'

Plus, he'd admitted *paperwork* took a lot of his time. But now, in the cold light of day, now she could see him properly, she realised how fully far-fetched her assumption had been. She glanced down and clocked his shoes. He wasn't wearing worn trainers like her, but leather loafers. Soft-looking, probably hand stitched, definitely expensive. Then she noticed the watch on his wrist. She didn't really know high-end watches, but the drivers wore them as part of their sponsorship deals, and this looked like one of those—expensive.

She was the biggest idiot on the planet. 'I thought you were someone who knew something of sacrifice. Of service. Of putting someone else first.'

'Didn't I do exactly that?' he murmured softly.

She hadn't meant *sex*. And while he'd seemed generous then, he was selfish as hell underneath.

'Sorry that I'm not the hero you wanted.' Bitterness darkened his eyes.

She didn't want or need a hero.

'You were only supposed to be the *cherry* on top of my perfect weekend,' she said stiffly. 'Instead, you've poisoned everything.'

All future possibility of her brand-new career. Because she hadn't hit the apex of a thrilling corner; she'd hit the apex predator himself. The most powerful guy in her world, who would kill her career with a blink.

He sighed. 'It's not that big of a deal—'

'No?' She flinched, stung by the dismissal even though she desperately wished she could agree. 'Then why didn't you tell me who you were before we...we...'

'Enjoyed ourselves?'

She had to acknowledge that she'd hardly been seduced. She'd been in the driver's seat with her foot flat hard on the accelerator. She'd barely spoken in those moments because she'd not wanted anything to stall those intense sensations. But what *he'd* held back had been serious.

She glared at him frigidly. 'Why lie?'

'I didn't lie. I certainly never said I was ex-services or a courier.'

But he'd omitted vitally important information and that *had* been deliberate.

'What exactly was your intention when for all that time you knew who I was?' she asked. 'When you knew all along that I *worked* for you?'

Massimo didn't know how his simple reconnaissance mission had exploded with such spectacular force. Fireworks were still going off inside him but he'd veered so far off course he couldn't find the way forward. All he could do was stare. Her hazel eyes flashed fire; her porcelain cheeks filled with reddened fury. She had every right to rage at him, but not everything that had happened had been *planned*. And he sure as hell had never been anyone's damned *cherry on top*. A little something juicy and sweet? That description suited her. Entirely.

For all his warnings to Emiliano, *he* was the one who'd messed up. Hell, he'd not acted on impulse like this in years. Now he couldn't even get her into the car to have this deeply awkward conversation in private. He'd lost all control and he wanted to start over. He wanted the *impossible*.

'If you get in the car, the driver will get out,' he muttered. 'At least we'll then have privacy while we talk and I'll answer all of your questions.'

She blinked. 'The driver gets out first.'

He supposed he couldn't blame her for being so mistrustful. A minute later Lily shot daggers at him as she climbed into the rear passenger seat and slammed the door behind her. Massimo took a moment to breathe before getting in from the other side, his body rebelling against the small distance between them. He'd only intended to find out about her. Instead, he'd devolved—dived head-long into the fastest, hottest sexual encounter of his life. He'd not lost control like that in years, and he was making it worse with every moment now.

'Why didn't you say anything?' she asked again. '*You* knew who I was, but you didn't think to be honest with me. Why not?'

Her biting tone spurred him into defensive mode. 'I was tired, I'd barely woken and you were practically in my lap and—'

'Are you suggesting you weren't capable of consent?' Her pupils flared and her cheeks flushed even more scarlet.

Oh no. He'd been *so* willing, because she'd been so overwhelming. She'd shredded his brain in a way that had never happened before and for that, in this instant, he blamed her. 'You kissed me first.'

'So I seduced you?'

'Didn't you?' It stung that she had such obvious regrets. 'You were the one who didn't want a brake point. You wanted us both to get the chequered flag.'

As fast as possible. And they had. And it had been worth it. Until now.

'That's true, I wanted that. I wanted *you*,' she acknowledged. 'Because I didn't know who you were. If I had, then I never—'

'I'll work something out,' he said hurriedly, not wanting to hear her vociferously reject him yet again. 'I'll arrange—'

The look on her face stopped him in his tracks.

'Are you *that* used to buying anything and everything you want?' She positively dripped with acerbic judgement.

Honestly, he didn't have to buy. These days he was *given* pretty much everything he wanted, *because* of the money he had. Money meant power and influence and control.

'You can't buy my silence.' She leaned forward. 'You can't buy *me*.'

'That was never my intention.' He did deals every damned day but somehow he couldn't see a way through this. Her proximity—her energy—smoked his ability to think.

'No?' She mocked him softly. 'But I bet you want my signature on an NDA. Isn't that what rich jerks like you do—contract your way out of trouble? Manage reputational risk with an oversize cheque here and there? Pay to make the *little problem* disappear?'

His lawyers might recommend that but as this was a first for Massimo, he didn't know and he wasn't about to ask them. And she wasn't a *little problem*; she was a damned bomb—

'Do you honestly imagine that I would ever want a single living soul to know what just happened between us?' She furiously exploded when he failed to answer. 'Do you think I want to sell my sky-high-sexcapade-with-a-billionaire story to the press?' She overflowed with scornful derision and kept spitting more. 'Do you think I'm going to blog about every amazing detail? Do—'

'I'm glad we agree it was amazing,' he interrupted coolly.

She gaped. Silenced. Good. His control trickled back. His clarity. He met her furious glare and felt the wicked need to be honest about something. Better late than never after all. 'It *was* amazing,' he repeated defiantly.

She could lay off the anger and outrage; he would do nothing to get in the way of her work. They could handle this like adults—calmly, rationally, reasonably. The bare fact of the matter was that he'd forgotten who he was for five minutes and he'd loved it. He'd been no one—just a guy in the dark with a girl. A traveller with no responsibilities and obligations, nothing but the freedom to do what he wanted. And he'd wanted her. Maybe she thought he'd used her and maybe he had, but she'd used him, too.

'I can only apologise for not telling you who I was sooner, but I genuinely lost track of everything when we were up there,' he said.

'You just wanted to get off.'

'Yes.' He refused to be ashamed of that. 'Same as you.'

She stared at him, clearly waiting for more. She was right to wait—he hadn't told her everything, but he could hardly admit he'd been trying to find out about her because he was worried about her intentions towards his teenage cousin. He'd been a fool. He did need to fix this. 'I can assure you that this won't affect your job—'

'You're right, it won't. Because I worked hard to earn my place in P1 Global. I earned it on merit and I'm *keeping* my spot.'

That was a fair point. He'd been consumed by desire; he'd let emotions cloud his judgement. From the moment he'd seen her in that damned video, he'd acted completely on impulse—something he'd not done in *years*.

'Why were you even on a cargo flight? Why weren't you on your fancy private jet?' She lifted her chin. 'How did you know my name?'

'I know all my employees' names.'

It was a lie, but he didn't want to admit why he knew

hers. Not confess he'd been there to quietly vet her motivations for being in the garage. That he'd considered her a threat to his cousin would only make her more angry and his suspicion *was* insulting. Even though where he came from, ulterior predatory motivations were totally common, she was hardly about to offer him any *poor little rich boy* pity. And he didn't want it.

'All five thousand of them? How very impressive,' she drawled sceptically. 'But you don't give a damn about workplace ethics or abusing your power.' Her gaze went right through him.

'I didn't abuse my power. You didn't know who *I* was. I didn't coerce you as your boss and I'm not going to now.' Even so, Massimo hadn't felt guilt like this in years. 'What happened isn't going to make a jot of difference to your job.'

'Because I'm too low level for you to bother with?'

'Lily—'

'*This* didn't happen,' she snarled suddenly. 'No one will *ever* know about this.'

He stared at her, ruthlessly suppressing his rising rebellion. The gulf of rejection. Who was she to dictate terms to him? He'd worked too hard for too long to gain complete control over his life, his family, his company. He'd not set a foot out of line in years. He'd been nothing but diligent and disciplined, driven to secure the family name, to recover the company, prove himself to those who'd disparaged him. Massimo owed it to his father. For all his failings, his father had fought so hard for him. But Massimo was not making the same mistakes. Only he just had—indulging in weakness for a beautiful woman.

'I don't want anything from you. Absolutely *nothing*

aside from your discretion. Do you understand?' Distress whitened her face. 'I'm not having the last five years of hard work wiped out by a single whisper of impropriety.'

He bit the inside of his cheek, waiting for her to finish.

'We'll never have anything to do with each other. We'll stay fifteen feet away from each other at all times.'

We. Her language linked them like a team, a couple. *Lovers*. Triumph flickered, reigniting his crazy attraction. She was a slight figure of fury and spellbinding with it.

'We'll never discuss it.' Her eyes glinted suspiciously. 'In fact, we'll never actually speak again. *Ever*.'

Despite it being justified, her judgement outraged him. Even though she was insisting on a protocol that he'd have demanded from her had he spoken first, he was utterly frustrated by the harsh rules she was imposing. Fully triggered, he didn't want to agree to her requirements. For the first time in years he wanted to rebel. To do what he *wanted*, not what was *expected*. But then giving in to that urge once tonight is what had him in this current untenable position.

Now she looked disturbingly pale. 'Do you agree?'

He gritted his teeth. 'Completely.'

'Then I'm out of here.'

But that last little thing Massimo *couldn't* agree to. 'I'll get out of the car. My driver will see you home safely.'

'That's not necessary.'

Of course she refused. Of course she was determined to have everything her own way—just as she'd had everything she'd wanted on that damned plane. But this time they didn't want the same thing.

'I've agreed to all your stipulations,' he said softly. 'Can't you concede this?'

Her gaze clashed—*locked*—with his and they both remained immobile. The smallest satisfaction swept through him. He could spend all day staring at her. Except her lips trembled, and regret coursed through him.

'You've travelled and worked long hours this week. It's Hearnshawe's responsibility to ensure you get home safe—' He broke off, realising it was the wrong thing to say.

She stiffened, outraged and independent to the end. 'I'm not and never will be *your* responsibility.'

CHAPTER FOUR

North Hamptonshire, England

NO ONE SAID ANYTHING. There were no whispers, no sly looks. No one seemed to *know.* Yet, every day Lily expected to be dragged off the factory floor on some trumped-up pretext and summarily dismissed. Just because he'd agreed to her stipulations at the time, didn't mean he'd stick to his word. People backtracked; they *betrayed.* Her parents, the people she ought to have been able to rely on more than anyone, had taught her that. In brutally ejecting her from the family, they'd destroyed her ability to trust anyone. And if Massimo Hearnshawe was ruthless enough to lock his own grandfather out of his office, he would definitely think nothing of dismissing her.

All she could do was keep her head down and hope Shane had enough integrity to give her a decent reference when the worst happened. And the really tragic thing was she was still naive enough to hope it might not. She'd gotten to work early, stayed late, studied in the evening to further upskill. Many of the technical crew had engineering degrees and she quietly wanted to prove herself as capable as all of them. Mostly, she needed to distract herself. But there was no ignoring the ripple of awareness as everyone's spine literally straightened late on Tuesday afternoon. Lily looked up, instantly wary. Massimo was making one of his rare appearances on the factory floor. She'd seen him here only once in the three months she'd been at Hearnshawe and even that had been from a distance. But today he walked right to her end of the room. Lily gripped her ratchet tightly, fearing butterfingers and fighting brainlessness.

'Shane?' Massimo called the chief mechanic over to join his entourage of engineers.

Too tense to breathe, Lily hoped she was hidden by the tool trolley, but she could see him. With his imposing height and haughty demeanour, he was in full CEO mode—impeccable suit, perfect tie, polished shoes. The contrast of his dark hair and his bright blue eyes was striking, as was that angular, clean-shaven jaw. He exuded authority, was better-looking than she'd dared not remember. But if he was aware of her, he didn't show it. He seemed engrossed in conversation with Shane as those engineers waited.

Consciously trying to regulate her breathing, trying to halt the flood of blood to her face, she forced herself to get back to work. Why was he here? Was this finally it—the moment of her total mortification? Her skin felt heat-rash prickly and she kept her head down. It was ten minutes of agony in which she got precisely nothing done. Finally, he moved off with that coterie of sycophants. Then Shane walked over to her.

'You'll be on the travel team for Belgium, Austria and Italy, followed by Singapore the week later,' he said. 'That okay?'

'Of course,' Lily squeaked, stunned. Why was he telling her this now?

Glancing beyond him she saw Massimo still too near, ostensibly talking to an engineer. The sight extinguished her flash of excitement. Had he told Shane to take her? To give her the best opportunities because *he* was afraid she was going to cause trouble in some way? Because that wasn't okay. For her to gain an advantage because she'd slept with him would be *worse* than losing her job.

She looked back at Shane, needing to test the horrible theory. 'Any chance for pit crew?'

It would be the peak of her career to perform the screamingly fast tyre changes. She'd mentioned it to Shane before and knew he saw her stature as a hindrance.

The chief mechanic hesitated. 'Keep working on strength. I know your speed is good.'

Not giving her everything, then. Reassured, she rallied. She would prove herself to Shane eventually. She would focus on her future, not that mistake in the dark; maybe the worst wasn't going to happen after all.

The four races Shane had listed meant she faced seven weeks of intensity before the mid-season break. As Massimo didn't travel to *every* race—not with all the companies he had to run—she might avoid him for much of that time. That prospect ought to be good, but as he left the factory she felt shockingly bereft.

She needed to get over herself—needed to stop wishing for something she'd never really had—because she still had to get through *this* weekend. It was their home race and Massimo would definitely be in attendance at that one. Fortunately, so would everyone else from the factory. There would be so many green team shirts and caps Lily could disappear into an amorphous mass of minions.

The next morning she went straight to the track to begin the pack-in with the rest of the garage crew. Less than an hour's drive from Hearnshawe headquarters, this circuit was where she'd worked in the junior karting leagues. She walked through the visitor centre on her way to the pit lane, studying the old honour boards on the way. Hearnshawe's history was entwined with the circuit, too. Fifteen years ago one young driver had dominated every year through the junior grades. *M. Hearnshawe* was listed six times as the winner before his name just disappeared. Lily, like everyone, knew that on a rainy afternoon Massimo's parents had died in a road accident not far from this very track. It was the year Massimo had vanished from the racing scene, only to emerge a decade later ousting his grandfather with that swift, savage coup. There'd been howls of disapproval over his vicious disrespect, but Massimo had defied all doubters and dragged Hearnshawe forward. He'd employed fresh talent and sourced serious investors, enabling rapid technological development. After years in the doldrums, Hearnshawe Racing was flying up the table in P1 Global. Conrad was consistently achieving podiums, and Emiliano's youth and innate talent had drawn millions of new fans. Which meant even more sales across the entire company brand—the licensed products were exceptionally popular, while their general auto sales were now stratospheric. While he'd improved every division within the conglomerate, Lily suspected Hearnshawe Racing was Massimo's true passion. Given his love of winning, she was surprised that he'd stopped driving entirely. Maybe he'd been ruthlessly fixated on gaining control of the company. He certainly had it now—he could get rid of her with a blink. That he hadn't still stunned her.

Despite the reassuring selection for the travel crew, Lily kept her head down throughout the weekend. Massimo would be in the suite, so she kept well away from there. During the race she held her breath as Emiliano and Conrad carved through the field, clawing back places after a disappointing qualifying result. The crowd roared, screaming for British success. Emiliano placed fifth while Conrad hit the podium in third. Swept along with her colleagues, Lily raced to watch the podium celebrations. Her willpower reduced in the excitement of success, she risked a glance towards the VIP section. She was so short, she figured no one would notice her looking the wrong way. While Massimo was so tall he was visible despite standing at the back, keeping his customary distance from the crowds.

He was looking directly at her. Not just looking, he was *locked* on her. Steely and solemn and heart-squeezingly heated. The noise, the people, the whole damned world, faded. Lily's smile froze as fragments of memory flickered and intense emotion surged. In the dark she'd focused on *touch*—relishing his hot, rough strength. His raw masculinity had roused something deeply primal in her. She'd tried telling herself that she'd fantasised it into something more than it really was—that it hadn't been *that* great—but in only *looking* at him now, lost in the brilliance of his blue eyes, her bones melted and her resistance evaporated. She was pinned in place, unable to break the invisible chains just his attention wrought around her. Worse, she couldn't help wistfully aching for *more*. His scrutiny didn't ease, his gaze didn't waver, he didn't move as for a blistering mad moment she was certain his thoughts mirrored hers. It never, ever could happen but she was trapped in an endless spell of searing longing.

'Amazing, right, Lils?'

One of the mechanics clapped her on the back, knocking her off balance. She stumbled, glancing down to keep her footing, and when she looked back to Massimo, he was gone.

Belgium

Massimo flew in last minute. He told himself he didn't want to miss Emiliano's first podium, and given his cousin's upwards trajectory, the chance of that happening at the Belgian race seemed likely. But that wasn't *entirely* why.

The social media team had worked a discreet miracle, flooding Emiliano's feed and seeding other accounts with enough content to bury that short clip of his interaction with the unidentified female. Massimo had checked Lily's online status personally. While all employees had a contractual stipulation not to bring the team into disrepute, Hearnshawe Racing employees *could* have a public social media account. The comms team even provided a roadmap with ideas and advice. But like Massimo, Lily Jones had neither private nor public social media accounts. She had no online presence at all. That fact had frustrated his weak moment of online stalking, but he'd found out further information in other ways. He now knew she worked long hours. He also knew this diligence had been her habit from the start so he couldn't flatter himself that her extra hours were in the hopes she might see him. Like everyone in the team, like him, she simply gave her all to the job.

Initially, he'd been glad Shane had given her a permanent place on the travel team. It meant he could work at headquarters without fear of bumping into her for all those away days. He'd tried not to look for her every time he walked through the factory in the past couple of weeks—which had been far more than was customary and necessary. He tried to ignore the random reasons his brain conjured to send him into the Belgian pit lane now. Because it wasn't his brain, it was his *groin* directing him. Basic lust. No matter how hard he tried, he couldn't forget those moments on the plane. Worse, the brief moment they'd had at the British race meant she now haunted him even more. He'd stood at the back and watched her sparkle as she'd celebrated Conrad's result with her colleagues. Then to his immense pleasure, she'd looked for *him*—because there was no other reason for her to glance *away* from the podium. But she'd caught him watching her and completely frozen. He'd felt guilty as fuck because he was quite sure what he'd wanted was written all over his face. And she'd been paralysed.

It was four weeks since that flight from Canada; surely, she was no longer worried she would suffer any ramifications because of what had happened between them. The only ramifications were impacting *him*. He felt the distance from her like a physical agony—it was as if he had the freaking flu. Frankly, he was furious about it.

But his last-minute arrival in Belgium had unforeseen repercussions. He'd forgotten Princess Celine—the highly photogenic social media darling and minor royalty from a nearby principality—was one of their VIP guests. Massimo couldn't decline her request for him to take her on a tour of their pit lane spot an hour before the race. He would stick to Emiliano's side of the garage, not risk an encounter with the lovely, forbidden Lily.

Unfortunately, Lily was the first person they saw, and Princess Celine was fascinated to discover a female mechanic on the floor. She swept towards her before Massimo could say anything. Surely, Lily wouldn't mind; there were so many damned witnesses it wasn't as if he was about to try anything inappropriate. He couldn't resist the chance to see her from a little fewer than her wretched fifteen-foot requirement.

Shane smoothly stepped forward to welcome them both and made introductions to all the team members present. The princess shook hands with them. Massimo numbly followed suit. His smile was set as stress rippled through every muscle. He'd not been this close to her in weeks. He wasn't supposed to get this close—*not* because it was what she'd requested, but to maintain control of *his* physical reaction to her. But he couldn't stop himself from studying her. Her hair was swept beneath that cap. The polo was loose on her slim frame. She looked pale, her fine features drawn. She shook hands with Celine, offered a slight answer to the question he'd not heard.

'You know Mr Hearnshawe of course,' Shane said to Lily.

'Of course,' Lily replied.

The chagrin in her glance stopped him in his tracks but there was no way to avoid touching her. He'd shaken hands with everyone else in the damned room. He stared, watching her whiten slightly as he offered his hand. There was a tiny hesitation before she put her hand in his. He immediately tensed, gripping her too tightly as an electrical charge shot up his arm. Shocked, he inhaled but with that, he caught her scent and then just held her hand longer. His whole body tensed. Gold flecks sparked in her hazel eyes and he finally felt her gently tug away. He immediately released her.

Hell. That brief contact had been too much, too long. He couldn't actually speak. But Lily could. She answered Celine's questions with a polite, deeply annoying level of acuity until Massimo finally recovered himself enough to suggest to the princess that they move out to inspect the track.

He escorted Celine away, turning his back on the sharpness in Lily's eyes as they left. He'd breached the boundaries she'd imposed. He'd stepped too close. But she needn't punish him—he was already truly suffering for it. He'd not wanted anyone the way he wanted her. And she didn't want a bar of him.

Conrad came third again with Emiliano closer than ever in fourth. This time, Massimo watched Lily at the podium celebrations safely from the suite. She wasn't sparkling this time. Maybe it was the screen but she looked paler than she had before the race. There was an almost desolate downturn to her mouth.

He frowned. Was she tired?

Austria

Lily religiously participated in every prerace team fitness routine. To make the pit crew, she had to hold her own strength-wise. Of course she was physically weaker than the guys, but that didn't mean she was *too* weak, so she showed up to any and every chance to prove herself. But on the morning of the Austrian race she felt atrocious. For the first time, there was no way she could run the track with the team.

It wasn't surprising she was exhausted; the weekend thus far had been hectic. Plus, her period was due. She wished it would hurry up so she could get her usual energy levels back; there was too much on the line for her to feel off.

She skipped breakfast at the hotel, but by mid-morning needed something to take away the gross taste in her mouth. The faint nausea was just nerves ahead of the race. On her break she went to the team trailer—a gleaming, three-storied paradise with private spaces for the drivers, a strategy room and VIP suites that also housed a team café. She walked in, about to scope the cabinet for a snack, when she saw Massimo at a corner table, a laptop open before him and a furrow between his brows. She stopped but it was too late. He glanced up and went stock-still but his blue gaze sharpened. What little appetite she had disappeared altogether as with one look she responded as if she was back on that plane. Her body remembered every small, snatched moment they'd shared in the darkness. She'd desperately wanted to forget it; instead, she was filled with the irresistible longing to walk over, slide onto his lap and lift her mouth for him to plunder. She didn't. She dragged in a shaky breath, trying to get control of herself.

Why was he working in here? Why was he at every race? It was horrific and so awfully unfair. Because she hopelessly, endlessly wanted to see him *more*, but he was the boss! More than that, he was so far out of her league—he entertained actual *princesses* like the one who'd been hanging off his arm in Belgium last week. The beauty was probably his new lover.

Strong wind suddenly rattled the windows, as if her bitter fury had manifested it. She backed out of the café and forced concentration; wind like this could impact the race hugely. She would snack later.

In the race Conrad placed second but to the team's disappointment, Emiliano's car had an engine fault and he was unable to finish.

'This was delivered for you, Lily.' Shane handed her a bag moments after the checkered flag fell.

Delivered by whom? Shane was gone before she could ask. Lily peeked inside the paper bag. Chocolate-covered almonds. Heat covered her in a whole-body blush. Her mouth watered—not in that horrible, nauseous way, but from hunger. Fortunately, everyone was going to the podium. Lily didn't. She stayed in the shadows and indulged in the sweet and thought of the one person in the world who knew she couldn't resist them.

Italy

As the Italian circuit was only five kilometres from Emiliano's birthplace, Massimo had a list of sponsor meetings the length of his arm, plus family obligations. But while the pressure on Emiliano was more intense than any other race on the calendar, Massimo kept an eye on the screen in the VIP suite as always.

In the final minutes of the qualifying session, Massimo was shocked to see Conrad spin out of control. Time slowed as he watched his driver slam into the safety barrier, sending debris all over the track. He froze. Waiting. But both image and sound on the screen were static. After an interminable few moments, the team radio crackled.

'I'm okay.' Conrad uttered the best words in the world. 'All good.'

Massimo exhaled sharply in relief. He stood as he watched Conrad climb out of the wreckage. He'd go straight to the medical centre and meet Conrad there.

He flexed his shoulders, trying to relax, but his own memory flashed. He remembered spinning like that, but the surface he'd been on had been slippery and wet. He'd not been in a P1 car, but a junior-level single-seater kart going nowhere near as fast as what Conrad had been travelling. Even so, the damage had been immense. Fortunately, there had been no rain here today. Conrad's rear wheels had locked up and while it was a *slow* collision, the impact still had severely damaged the car. Massimo knew that if Conrad was okay and cleared by the doctors, he would still want to race tomorrow. Which meant Lily faced a long night of repairs with the other mechanics.

He'd not seen her since she'd come to the café in Austria. He'd looked into her eyes—a kaleidoscope of green, brown and gold before she'd blinked and backed away. He'd kept the required distance but had sent her the almonds. She'd looked like she needed the nutrition, but he hoped he'd provoked her memory as well. His memory of her was driving him insane. Did she think of those moments on the plane as he so damned often did?

He was never going to know because she acted as if he didn't exist. For Massimo Hearnshawe, this was something of a novelty. She never looked at him, which he knew, because he couldn't stop looking at her. He was increasingly drawn nearer when it should be getting easier to stay away. Where that night he'd appreciated his anonymity, now his apparent invisibility was an irritant. Of course she was within her rights not to want him, except he didn't want to think that was the case.

Surely, he'd not dreamed that heat in her eyes.

He worked through the night, shortening his action list in the hotel room, trying not to think about Lily working through piecing Conrad's car back together. He couldn't allow this distraction to ruin everything, not when he'd finally gotten Hearnshawe Racing to be capable of *winning*.

In the morning he worked in the VIP suite, keeping an eye on the prerace coverage, hoping for a glimpse into the garage that didn't come. With a growl he pushed away from his desk and went in search of coffee. He needed a break from the intensity of back-to-back meetings broken by intrusive thoughts regarding Lily. He stalked to the team café. Someone had left a bunch of Hearnshawe uniforms in a pile on a chair in the corridor. But as he passed, the pile moved. He stopped, stunned to see it wasn't a pile of clothing at all, but a small figure curled up on the chair. Lily Jones was fast asleep. He stared down at her, unable to breathe in case he woke her, unable to drag himself away.

Her skin was as creamy as ever, if anything more translucent, but her fine features seemed sharper. Her long lashes rested on those delicate high cheekbones and there were shadows and hollows that were new. Her full lips were slightly turned down, almost as pale as the rest of her. His fingertips tingled; the desire to trace her features was almost irresistible.

Massimo curled his fingers into fists. He knew exactly how he could bring her colour back, but she was no fairy-tale princess needing waking with a kiss, and he was no Prince Charming. He wanted her fully awake and wholly willing when he kissed her again. Not that it could ever happen. Bracing, he leaned back against the opposite wall. Keeping his distance from her as he'd promised he would, but equally unable to leave her alone. Not when she was this vulnerable. Hell, he had such a damned fixation on her.

He heard a footstep in the corridor and moved to block the way, putting his finger to his lips. 'Don't wake her.'

Shane looked startled. But then Massimo didn't usually growl at him.

'She can have five more minutes. No one needs to know,' he added with a gentler whisper.

'Of course.' Shane immediately turned, but was clearly stunned that the CEO of Hearnshawe Racing was watching a mechanic literally sleep on the job.

Massimo resumed his watch over her, barely unable to cage the temptation rising within him. She was clearly working too hard. It had been a tough few weeks for everyone, but none of the other mechanics had fallen asleep in a busy corridor less than an hour before a race. She shouldn't be this pale, either. And he shouldn't be craving the impossible. He was fed up—with Conrad's crash, the stress of deals he needed to do, Lily's exhaustion. It was too much.

She finally stirred and he silently stepped back, returning to the stream of people waiting for him in the suite. But that sad tilt to her mouth lingered in his mind.

During the race Conrad made up several places from

the back of the field, proving his talent and the speed of the car and rewarding the effort of the team who'd worked through the night. Emiliano was easily within the top ten. But Massimo kept thinking about Lily. Was she unwell? Were the long hours getting to her? Was she lonely with this lifestyle? Was that why she'd been tempted to have that stolen moment with a stranger? Had it been a secret need expressed—a physical release that she had no other time for? She *should* have more. She should have some lucky guy waiting at home to help her unwind.

Massimo gritted his teeth at the thought. He felt unreasonably jealous just seeing other mechanics talk to her. Relationships within the company were discouraged, but maybe he'd finally forget her if she *were* involved with someone else.

'We should have drinks or something,' he murmured to Andre after the race. 'A mid-season celebration to thank the travel team for all their hard work.'

Andre gaped, unable to mask his surprise. 'Okay, when are you thinking?'

'Before the break would be good. Singapore?' Far away from Hearnshawe headquarters. Maybe he might actually see her smile from a distance. 'It'll be hot. They'll need some relief. Could be a reward once the setup is complete on Wednesday night?'

'Drivers won't be there,' Andre pointed out.

'That's a good thing.' Massimo quelled his jealousy again. 'Surely, there's a singer wanting pit lane access who'll perform?'

'I'll get onto it right away.'

CHAPTER FIVE

Singapore

LILY TRIED TO focus on the verdant greenery, not her conflicting feelings. She'd checked the footage from the past few years and Singapore was the one race Massimo never attended, so she could relax and enjoy the week. They'd arrived yesterday to give them time to acclimatise and had spent the afternoon exploring before dining at the hotel. It was glorious—she'd been fascinated by the contrast of the soaring modern skyscrapers and the decoratively ornate temples. But Singapore was the most physically gruelling race on the P1 Global calendar. There were several layers of added complexity. It was a street track, not a purpose-built circuit, so overtaking was difficult and there weren't just barriers, but solid walls that left even less room for error. Then there was the heat and humidity—the sessions and race were actually held at night when it was slightly cooler. Lily never experienced temperatures like this. No wonder several of the drivers flew in last thing and went straight to air-conditioned hotels, emerging enveloped in ice packs and constantly taking on liquids just in time to get into the cars.

Lily needed to prepare better for the race weeks in general. She'd fully embarrassed herself by falling asleep in the corridor not long before the race in Italy. It was appalling. She'd not worked as late as some of the others that night and they'd still managed to stay awake. Fortunately, she didn't think she'd been out long and no one said anything when she went back. But only ten minutes into the prep in the pit lane, her stomach tilted, churning the meagre breakfast she'd managed at the hotel. Coping with the hot weather, she was not.

'Are you okay?' Shane glared at her.

'Yes,' she muttered. Vision swimming, she was seeing two Shanes and neither looked happy. 'I'm fine.'

Her boss pointed to the door. 'Out. Now. You're not infecting the rest of us.'

'No, it's not a bug,' she argued. 'It's something I've eaten or maybe it's the heat.'

'We all ate at the same restaurant last night and we're all okay. Scram back to the hotel and get some rest. If you're better later, come to the party, otherwise quarantine in your hotel room, understood?'

'I don't need to come to the party.'

'*Everyone* needs to come to the party,' Shane muttered. 'It's team bonding. Go now. I need you well. This week is tough enough.'

He was right and others were watching. No one else wanted to be sick and she definitely wouldn't want to infect the drivers if it was a bug. Which it wasn't. But it couldn't be food poisoning, because Shane was right about them eating at the same restaurant. It was just the heat. She needed an intensive recovery plan. Electrolytes, painkillers and a brief nap in her air-conditioned hotel room.

She slept for five hours straight and felt better on waking. Relieved, she showered and dressed in the dress she'd brought with her for the party. She'd not had a night out in *years*. Basically ever. And it would be a work event *without* Massimo. That was good, right? She paired her dress with strappy sandals; its length made her look taller than she was. It was too hot to wear her hair down, so she swept it into a bun and then put on the thin sterling silver pendant she'd bought when she'd made it to P1 Global. She was late, but definitely still showing up.

The Hearnshawe party was in one of the elite entertainment facilities next to the Singapore Flyer. Lanterns lit the way and the sky was a stunning colour, but the air was so close and warm she had to walk slowly. Frankly, after only five minutes outside she felt rocky again. It was *definitely* heat related. She would need an ice pack in the garage tomorrow. Except she didn't only feel *tired*, she also felt nauseated—an echo of the constant queasiness she'd felt a couple of weeks ago. Which was weird. What sort of bug caused intermittent symptoms like that?

Her brain slowly whirred and for the first time in weeks she let herself focus on her body—trying to feel in tune with it. Not only was there that damned endless ache for Massimo, there was also something else. Something deeply sensitive, something terrifying. Suddenly dizzy, she spun, consumed with the need to escape, but slammed into something hard. Firm hands hit her shoulders. *Familiar* hands that softened and shaped, holding her gently. She jerked her head up.

'What are you doing here?' she squeaked.

'You're late,' he muttered.

'What?' Stunned he'd materialised just as she'd thought of him, she struggled to understand. 'I'm *what*?'

'Late.' His tone censured her and something like reproach burned in the backs of his eyes.

He thought she was late to the party, but she was also late in a deeply personal way. How could she not have realised sooner? Now she gaped as the horrifying truth hit. She'd dismissed it as travel sickness. That her fatigue was simply stress. But this wasn't a bug, this was a baby.

No!

'I thought you weren't coming,' he added huskily.

She blinked. She was freaking herself out. She went through irregular patches. They'd used protection. She was overcooked by the heat and delirium had set in.

His bright blue eyes bored into her with concern he had no right to feel. That *she* had no right to appreciate. Trying not to react, she dropped her gaze only to drink in his hewn physique. In the pale linen he looked impossibly cool and she was almost overcome by the yearning to lean against him. Her nipples tightened. Her body didn't care about what her brain was computing. Her body just wanted his—like an animal recognising her mate.

'Lily?' His hands tightened again. 'You're not feeling better, are you?'

Her gaze shot back to his. How did he know she'd been feeling off colour? Had Shane told him?

'You fell asleep before the last race—you're working too hard.'

How did he know about *that*? Completely mute, she shook her head, never as mortified. She wasn't *weak*. She was—

'Are you sure you're well enough to be here?'

He was right in front of her and she was reacting in the most inappropriate manner imaginable. It was as if he'd been imprinted on her in a purely animal way. Before she'd known who he was, she'd felt him, she'd let him in and that part of her was now so thrilled to see him she was basically a molten puddle at his feet.

'Don't you want me to be here?' she asked.

'Not if you're unwell.' He frowned and actually put the back of his hand to her forehead. 'You're flushed.'

Because she got *hot* around him! And she had to get away from him now. 'My health isn't any of your business.'

Except maybe part of it was. She lost her ability to breathe and focused on fury instead. Why was he here? Why was he breaking their fifteen-feet-away agreement? Overcharged and overwhelmed, every emotion overtook her.

'Lily, you're not—'

'I'm fine,' she snapped, her words hurtling faster than the cars on track. 'In fact, I'm more than fine. In fact, I think I'm *pregnant*.'

Time stopped as he stared into her face. Reading her rage, her *blame*. And while she'd been exhausted a second ago, now she was invigorated. His presence—his proximity—was suddenly like a shot in the arm. She pushed away from him and turned. Too late, she saw the people. Mechanics, engineers, marketing team—all with glasses and platters and this was a horrifically public setting in which to have a deeply private conversation. She couldn't be seen talking intimately with the CE Bloody O! There was no reason for her ever to talk with him. Had anyone else *heard* her? She blinked furiously as her vision muddied, multiplying the number of people around her until they looked like a drunken choir of judgemental bystanders.

Massimo grabbed her hand and walked her in another direction, the rapidity of his movements conveying the strength of his emotions. She was so stunned she was just swept along; she didn't even see where they were going. All she knew was that it was suddenly, blessedly cooler.

'Forgive me. You'll need to get the next one,' he growled as they passed a group of people. 'She needs cool air and space.'

'What are you doing? Where—'

Lily broke off as she saw the door had closed and they were alone in a glass compartment. She gasped as the compartment moved, leaving that pile of people behind. He'd taken her into the Singapore Flyer—the enormous Ferris wheel with the stunning views of Singapore city that she'd not had the chance to check out yet. But they were trapped for the next twenty minutes or more and his high-handed behaviour was appalling. '*Loads* of people could fit in here, but you're spoilt enough to take one entirely to yourself?'

'I'm not by myself. You're here with me. And you do need space.'

This was an argument easier to face than the one that really mattered. 'They've been *queuing*—'

'Not for that long. This is a private event.'

He'd caused a scene and she was mortified and definitely didn't want to consider what she'd so brainlessly blurted. 'You made me look weak in front of everyone.'

'Right now you *are* weak. Sit down before you fall down. Your face is whiter than your dress.'

She sat on the wide bench seat in the centre of the compartment. He didn't. He stared down at her from his imposing height.

'I need you to repeat what you said a couple of minutes ago.'

She'd spoken before thinking. She still wasn't thinking and she really didn't want to believe—

'Do you think or do you *know*?' he gritted impatiently.

She gripped her hands together. 'I don't know. I just...'

'*Know?*' he said softly. Sceptically.

She pressed her fists to her stomach. Her breasts were more tender, which could be premenstrual, but she counted back and she was more than a *little* late. She suddenly stood. She needed to get out of here. She needed to process this alone. But the world's fanciest Ferris wheel was taking forever to spin all the way around. She glanced at the stunning skyline before looking to the brightly lit track below. Five kilometres of high-speed circuit. She would give anything to be in a car right now, racing at such high speed there'd be no room to think about anything else.

'And you think it's mine?' Massimo asked even more sceptically.

She turned and stared at him vacantly. Of course it was his. Why was he asking that...?

Oh. She suddenly felt winded. *Wounded.* All these weeks she'd been pining—thinking, hoping, *dreaming* that he felt a little bit the same every time he saw her at work. That he watched her, wanted her, thought of her the way she did him. But no. He'd been entertaining *princesses* and who knew who else.

Right. But it felt so *wrong*.

She supposed she couldn't blame him for thinking there might be alternatives given she'd slept with him after a five-minute conversation. For all he knew, she'd slept with a different stranger every other night since that flight. He probably had. He liked to move fast. She was shockingly miserable at the thought.

'There are no other possibilities?' he added, twisting the knife.

'Not that I can think of right now.' Her words were strangled.

He was the only man she'd had sex with in the past five years.

He didn't seem pleased about it. His eyes narrowed. 'If you've had symptoms for a while, why haven't you done a test? It's weeks since that flight from Canada. Surely, you've checked?'

'I've been busy. I thought…' She'd been hiding from *herself*—burying in long workdays and late study, then sleeping like the dead. She'd been trying everything not to think of him and those few hours they'd shared, trying to ignore the achy yearnings of her treacherous body. And she'd been such a *fool*—because he'd clearly not been thinking of her at all.

Like her family didn't think of her. Or her ex. Or anyone.

'So we're having a baby.'

She closed her eyes to buy herself some emotional distance and hurriedly reconstruct her spine. She *desperately* needed more defence.

'Lily?' He sounded so much closer.

She blinked and stepped back to the window. Turned to look out it to hide her distress. The lights were dazzling. Everything outside was slowly spinning, but inside her panic was increasing. Her heart hammered off beat and too fast. She was unable to focus properly, because now he was near and her weak body just wanted. Horrified by his apparent irresistibility, *flippancy* was her only self-protection.

'I guess we burned through the rubber,' she murmured. 'Got a puncture. Lost control and spun out on turn one.'

She turned to read his expression and found him right in front of her. Icily serious. Right. It was hardly the time to be making weak P1 puns.

'What's your strategy here?' he asked, not just cool, frigid.

She shivered, unwilling and unable to face the full implications of this mess. She didn't want to deal with it. She just wanted to forget everything, bury her head in bliss. And here he was—her *source* of bliss. She tried to brake but her body was feeling everything too fast—melting in that inexorable slippery slide towards him. Sexual magnetism at its most extreme. Hormones? Not only those. She'd wanted nothing but him for weeks and now he was close enough to kiss her and she desperately, dreadfully wished he would.

'Lily?'

They were toe to toe but she yearned for him to step closer still. She had to hold herself utterly still as inside, shooting sparks of attraction spiralled through to her core—to where she was hottest. Hungriest.

His impatience grew more visible the longer she remained silent. 'What is it you think you're going to *win*?'

In a vague corner of his stunned brain, Massimo knew he shouldn't use his size to dominate her petite stature.

Nor should he feel this roaring satisfaction at having some small semblance of power over her, but he was too furious to give a damn. He needed the advantage in this one wild second as proprietary—predatory—instinct flared. Was she pregnant? Because if she was… *If* she was…

He couldn't *think*.

But her silence, her superficial glibness, made him pause. Why was she acting as if this was some kind of *game*? Why let something so monumental just slip out and then joke about it? He suppressed his possessive impulses and tried to analyse because it didn't add up. He knew she was hard-working, driven… *Ambitious.*

Of course.

Bitter disappointment roared. He'd thought she was different—that she truly didn't want anything from him. But she did. Same old thing. Too bad. He wasn't letting an innocent *child* be used in a shakedown for money.

He'd been such a fool. He'd actually organised this party as a self-torturous pretext to see her. He'd been so disappointed when she'd not arrived that he'd had to pace away from everyone. Then she'd appeared like an ethereal nymph, gliding towards the crowd in a long white dress with wafer-thin straps and bodice that cupped her breasts. She looked stunningly sweet and sexy and he'd had to intercept her. Except not only had she not seen him, she'd also smacked into him. He'd gotten a hit of her fresh scent. He inhaled another now, just as he was trying to clear his head and regain his wits.

'What do you mean *win*?' she questioned thinly.

As rare as his sexual encounters were, he always paid relentless attention to contraception. It *shouldn't* have failed. But then it had been an age since he'd needed contraception. The condom had probably been ancient—failure was entirely possible.

But how did he know there hadn't been ten guys since him? Any one could be the father. He shouldn't take her word for it. Only he didn't want to think about her expression when he'd straight out asked her if there'd been someone else. Her eyes had widened as if she'd been shocked. But then—worse—she'd almost looked bereft. He was angry that he'd hurt her with that question. He shouldn't have the power to hurt her. She couldn't—shouldn't—care. There just couldn't be any of this complication. And what was with the wild impulse pushing him to pull her close and kiss her and tell her everything was going to be all right? He quelled it furiously.

He was used to making fast decisions. Responsibility for almost everything rested with him and he'd grown the shoulders for it. He couldn't just abandon an obviously emotional woman. He needed to ensure she got back to her hotel safely and at least find out for certain if she was pregnant and then if it was his—

He gritted his teeth. He'd never wanted to marry, nor have a family, despite societal expectation. He'd figured Emiliano would be his heir. But now? With icy fury he knew exactly what he was going to do. *If* she was pregnant, *if* it was his, then there was only one tolerable outcome. Yet, in his gut he knew there were no *ifs*; both those things were true. With a sinking feeling he wondered whether she would try to retract her claim when he informed her of their future.

'What do you mean by *strategy*?' she added, her fury becoming more audible.

'Why you've held this news back. Why you've decided to make your move here and now.' So publicly. So shockingly.

His doubts ought to destroy the desire thrumming through him, yet he found himself leaning closer to study her shadowed eyes. He remembered the silky softness of her skin, her warmth.

'My *move*?' Her head tilted as she studied him. 'Do you think I planned this?'

'Didn't you? Not the pregnancy itself, but you've certainly taken time to consider your options. Have you been waiting for the perfect moment to spring it on me? Is that why you're here?'

She gaped. 'Are you so arrogant to think that you're the only reason I want to stay working at Hearnshawe? Do you think that I didn't mean it when I said we weren't to talk again? I'm here. To *work*.'

He was barely thinking at all right now. He just needed to clutch. 'Let's go. We'll make the arrangements,' he said huskily.

'Arrangements for…?'

'Pregnancy test. Paternity. If they're positive, we'll get married.'

'*What?*'

'If you're pregnant. If it's mine. Then we're getting married.'

He figured she'd either leap at the proposal or push for money. It was only a matter of which.

She glared up at him. 'For all you know I might not even keep the baby.'

Rage ripped into every muscle, bunching them and making him lean closer still. If there was one thing he would do in the rest of his life, it was ensure this baby thrived. 'No problem. I'd love full custody,' he lied. 'I'll get my lawyer on a call and we'll whip up a contract right now.'

She stood her ground. 'You're *never* having custody of *my* baby.'

Insulting yet oddly rewarding. Her fire partially eased the icy chunk within that had been so disappointed in her. Yet, he couldn't stop testing her motives. 'Why not? Do you want to keep it because of the money you think will come with it?'

Her nostrils flared. 'You're unbelievably insulting.'

'Perhaps. But you need to understand that I'm not going to pay you off. You won't get millions to live the high life. If this baby is mine, I'll be a fully involved father and for that to happen, *you'll* be my wife.'

He'd proposed in an impetuous fit of fury but now he rage-warmed to the idea. If she was going to throw a bomb in his life, he'd throw one right back. 'You'll be stuck with me. Illegitimacy is not an option.'

He'd endured the whisperings even after his parents had married. While he no longer cared what anyone thought of him, his *child* wasn't facing that.

'What is this, the nineteen-hundreds?' she questioned scathingly. 'You don't need to save my reputation and certainly not the baby's. The child can take your name but I don't want to. And you certainly don't need to feel as if you have to be *fully involved*.'

Had she heard his underlying discomfort at the prospect of paternity?

'Don't feel as if you have to do the *right thing* by me.' Her caustic words confirmed his suspicion. 'I can manage on my own just fine. I don't want a cent of your money.'

'Why? Is it somehow worth less than other money?' he muttered, his anger easing the more hers was roused. 'You have several million of your own hidden away? An offshore account?'

'Don't be facetious.' She tossed her head up defiantly. 'I don't need it and I don't want it.'

She was a petite, ferociously independent lioness but she was still pale and *trembling*. What the hell was he doing fighting with her? Why was he bullying her with a rear-guard random proposal he wanted as little as she?

Guilt hit. A whole bunch of contrary emotions chopped up his insides. This situation was abominable. He couldn't understand how the hell any of it had happened. He stared while she gleamed like a furious damned diamond in the flickering lights. Gold flecks sparkled in her eyes. Energy streamed from her, merging with the electricity thrumming through him. He wanted to forget it all. To press close and hit oblivion with her. But he couldn't. He had to explain.

'I was born before my parents married. It led to some issues.' He wasn't having this child face any doubts over lineage. Nor did he want it to suffer from the family pressure and ironically, it was safer to protect it from *within* the family fold. It would mean Massimo could actually keep a better distance. He had a knack for employing very good staff. He'd been able to protect Emiliano well enough that way; he would do the same for this child. And for Lily herself. Because *he* couldn't get *too* close. He would fail if he got too close, just as he'd failed his parents. He'd failed his baby brother.

'I'm sorry you experienced issues *years ago*,' she said sarcastically. 'But the *world* has changed.'

He smiled bitterly. 'Not *my* world. Legitimacy matters. Especially for a family like mine. This child must be seen as my rightful heir.'

'To your great empire?' Weirdly, she whitened all over again. 'You have no idea who *I* am. No idea where I've come from.'

'I know you're a hard worker. You're focused. You're driven. You wouldn't be working in P1 Global if you weren't and certainly not for Hearnshawe Racing. That you've been selected and successfully working for us tells me all I need to know.'

She didn't take it as a compliment. 'Because only the *best* work for you?'

He nodded, unashamedly. 'We can work out any other problems as they arise.'

'You're not listening to me. You're ludicrously wealthy. I'm not.' She stiffened. 'I'm not from a suitable background.'

'What is this, the nineteen-hundreds?' he mocked. 'Class and social division are irrelevant.'

'Because you say so? Yet, some old-fashioned notion about illegitimacy is important enough to wreck both our lives? You really do live in another world, don't you?'

Yes, maybe he did.

'Can there be no conversation, no compromise possible?' She registered his implacability. 'No. You've gone straight to dictator mode. Well, you're going to have to level up even more and go full gangster to get your wish.' She goaded him. 'Go on, steal my passport. Gag me and drag me up the aisle. Drug me. That's what it's going to take because there is nothing you can do or say that would make me agree to marry you.'

He suddenly smiled, enjoying her rebellion. 'I think I can convince you. I've gotten you to say yes before. I've gotten you to scream it.'

'You want to seduce me into doing your bidding? Go right ahead—screw me till I can't stand. You have my full permission to touch me wherever, however, you want.'

She was outrageous fire and determination. She ran so hot so quick and he relished the pure provocative challenge she'd just thrown at him. Somehow, this had gone off course, but he recognised her steely beauty. She wasn't backing down. Nor was he. Breathless, furious, he was desperate to touch her again and avoid thinking about everything else.

'Thank you for that,' he growled. 'I won't forget.'

'No problem.' She tossed her chin up and whispered in his ear, so tantalisingly close. 'But I will *never* say yes to marrying you.'

'Never say never, Lily.'

As much as he wanted to sweep his hands over her body and make her shake, they were in a glass cage. As it was he was too close to her for comfort given the occupants of the opposite compartments could see their silhouettes. He could use that fact, of course. Publicly confirm their relationship, but if he touched her now, he mightn't be able to stop. Yet, nor could he step back.

An agonised expression flickered in her eyes. Triumph surged, tempting him even more. Oh how he ached to wreak vengeance on her for holding him at such lengths for so long. *He'd* been trying so hard to be good for freaking ever. He'd burned with frustration and now she was finally here, clearly as drawn to him as he was to her and he was so close to losing control. But this was no longer about just the two of them. There was something more important to consider. More terrifying.

'I can't indulge you here, darling.' He forced himself to move. Away.

Her eyes widened with surprise and she ducked her head.

'We're nearly back down.' Her voice caught. 'I'll go back to the hotel and find out for sure.'

'I'll come with you,' he said swiftly.

'No. We are not causing more drama.'

For once in his life he didn't give a damn about drama. She looked dangerously pale again and he was not abandoning her. 'You're unwell. I'm merely being a wonderfully supportive employer and ensuring that you're looked after.'

'I can get a—'

'Stop arguing. Start accepting.'

Her cheeks flushed with fury. Good. He preferred it to the pallor and the panic.

It took only moments for them to discreetly escape. His driver easily found an open pharmacy. Massimo strode in and bought the necessary and they carried on to her hotel. Her room was too small, the bed too big. He turned, noting her small case and the fat notebook on top of it. Lily went into her bathroom. Massimo barely had time to draw breath before she returned.

'We definitely have a situation.' She set the test on the small table. 'I don't want anything from you. I need time to think.'

He was more than happy for her to have that. He needed it, too. But she would be accepting so *much* more from him if this was his. Only there definitely was no *if.*

It hadn't even occurred to her that she could escape the apparent horrors of his proposal by suggesting someone else was the father and she just didn't have that in her.

For most people this would be a cause for *celebration.* He remembered his mother's happiness when she'd told him she was pregnant. She and his father hadn't told him right away. Massimo had only realised years later just how long they'd been trying, how nervous they were. They'd waited a few months to be sure all was well. That was why they'd been able to tell him he'd be getting a little brother in five months' time. He'd barely listened to them that day; he'd only teased his mother that her tears were falling faster than the rain outside—

He gritted his teeth. He couldn't be responsible for harm coming to another pregnant woman. He wouldn't just take care of Lily. He would take care of *everything.*

'If I leave you for the night, you won't run away?' He suddenly worried she would. He didn't want her acting on *emotion.*

'Of course not.' She gaped at him. 'There's a race this weekend.'

He bit the inside of his cheek to stop himself informing her that she would *not* be working. 'This is my personal number. Any problem through the night, call me.' His annoyance rebuilt when she looked at it as if it were poison. 'I'll send a car for you in the morning and we'll talk.'

And she wouldn't be working.

'I'm perfectly capable of getting to the track.'

'No.' He glared at her. 'I'll come and get you.'

She frowned. 'From where?' Her eyes narrowed. 'Are you not staying in *this* hotel?' She blinked. 'Is it not luxurious enough for you?'

He was in an exclusive suite at a premier hotel and stupidly, instantly, got defensive about it. 'You're the one who insisted on us being at least fifteen feet away.'

'You don't trust yourself to be in the same hotel as me?'

'That's right.' The hot and wild sensation in his gut goaded him to provoke her. 'But given the situation, maybe it would be easier if I stayed here tonight.'

Fury sparked in her eyes. 'You're *not* staying in my room.'

He relished her passion, but clung on to enough reason to remind himself she wasn't just tired. She was shocked and emotionally overwrought and in no state to make decisions. No. He needed to step back, recover his own reason. So he fell back on the teasing banter that had first brought them together all those weeks ago.

'Oh Lily,' he murmured. 'Are you rescinding my access-all-areas pass already?'

CHAPTER SIX

LILY DRESSED IN her team polo and shorts and turned her back on the test still on the table. Even so, the double stripes taunted her. Definitely *pregnant*. To her astonishment she'd fallen asleep almost the second she hit the pillow, but she'd woken early. She would head to the track and bury herself in work. Full ostrich mode. She didn't have the time or the emotional capacity to process the pregnancy let alone make a plan. She couldn't deal with something so monumental. It was so life altering, so terrifying, she had to stall even thinking about it.

'Are you well enough to be here?' Shane frowned at her when she walked into the garage.

'Absolutely.' The focus required would help steady her fraught nerves.

'I didn't see you at the party.'

'I was there briefly.' Most of the time she'd been in the Flyer having the worst conversation of her life with her boss.

Massimo had been such a jerk. She couldn't believe he'd coldly insinuated she'd want to milk him for his money. As if she'd want to take advantage of a *baby* in that way? Was the child not real to him? Or was it just a thing—another possession like his many cars and companies? That he'd obviously had other lovers since her, and thought she had, too, also rankled. Even though he was well within his right to, the thought infuriated her. He'd been as *heartless* as he'd been territorial. But he'd come alive when she'd snapped back at him. Of course he liked a challenge. He was in the top one percent, the absolute elite in the world. With his outsize ego and outsize drive, he lived a different life from normal—especially with the enormous wealth he'd inherited, then compounded. He could buy anything he wanted, but most of the time he didn't have to because sycophants and sponsors and celebrities wanted his grace and favour and attention. Therefore, *no* wasn't a word he heard. He hadn't liked it, but he was going to have to get used to hearing it from her. His attempt to control everything angered her most. He'd unleashed his inner Medieval overlord. But Lily would never let someone dictate what happened in *her* life— certainly not something as important as this.

His outrageous *proposal* had been a spur-of-the-moment reaction, thinking it was the *done thing.* She wouldn't let him move so damned fast that she didn't have the chance to catch her breath or use her brain. He would change his mind once he knew the truth, *especially* if respectability really mattered to him. Which meant she needed to tell him the second she saw him again. It would be more shameful to marry her than to pay her off. The man hung out with princesses, so once he knew the extent of her unsuitability, he would back away and be grateful for his lucky escape. It wasn't as if his proposal had been underpinned by any actual interest. He'd hardly rushed to take up her offer to seduce her any time he liked. The tragic thing was she'd wanted him to. She couldn't believe one wilful part deep inside her was disappointed that he'd left her alone last night. Here she was, facing a life-changing, shocking situation and all she really cared about was that he'd not kissed her again. She was pathetic. Crazy. Both.

At some point she would need to stop and absorb the fact that in only a few months she would become a mother with a baby to nurture and protect. Her mother hadn't mothered her. Neither of her parents had loved her in the unconditional way they were supposed to. Lily had focused on building a life for herself, all but alone for the past five years. Honestly, it had been going pretty well. But whether the life she'd built would be good enough to bring a baby into—whether *Lily* herself would be good enough—that she didn't know. The thought of failing *terrified* her.

She would try, she would be *better* than they'd been, but she had to retain her independence from Massimo. Marrying him—trying to create a family unit—wasn't going to happen. She'd believed in her family only to find the foundation had been brittle—shattering beneath pressure. She would never create a *false* foundation when it, too, could be pulled from her at any moment. She *was* alone in this.

Heartsore, she hunched down by the cabinets, checking over the tools, keeping her mind too busy to worry more. Thursdays in race week were a hive of activity. The pit crew practised tyre changes over and over. Engineers studied endless data streams from the simulations. There were musicians practising, vendors setting up food stalls with huge amounts of supplies, media people everywhere and VIP fans with passes and phones.

She'd barely gotten into it when Shane walked over. 'We've been asked to send a client out on a few reconnaissance laps.'

Lily nodded. Sponsor and celebrity encounters were super important. Hearnshawe Racing wasn't just about winning; they had luxury cars to sell. Endorsements and experiences maintained their brand name and recognition. 'You want me to take him around the circuit?'

'We have permission from the stewards. I just need a driver.'

Lily chuckled lightly. 'But it's not a hot lap?'

'You wish.' Shane laughed. 'No. All you have to do is point out the features of the track and the car. I figured you might want to get out of the heat for ten minutes. Just watch for the incoming rain.'

Cruising around in an air-conditioned Hearnshawe coupe definitely sounded like a nice way to spend some time, and she already knew any rain wasn't going to lower the temps. It would just slow them down—which meant even longer in the car and that was a good thing. P1 Global drivers were often born into the scene—Emiliano was a prime example. Aside from his aunt marrying into the Hearnshawe dynasty, he was a direct descendent of a long line of Italian racing drivers. Even Conrad was second generation. But Lily was also born into a racing family. She knew how to get around the streets quickly. Not that there would be the chance to drift and truly burn rubber here. But as she greeted the client and then strapped into the supremely luxurious vehicle, she felt that promise of freedom that only high speeds offered.

Massimo arrived at the track in a high temper and full of regrets. The sudden downpour of torrential rain soured his mood more. He should've gone with animal instinct and stayed with her last night. Instead, he'd tried to respect her boundaries. Tried not to act on impulse any more than he already had with her. He still couldn't believe he'd effectively proposed, but he'd been too provoked to argue with her to walk it back. Even though he didn't want to marry, it *would be* the right thing to do. He'd gone over it and over it the entire night—had precisely zero sleep—and still circled back to the same damned conclusion.

When he'd returned to her hotel early this morning, she'd already left. Now the rain drummed loudly on the roof, impeding his already compromised ability to cope. If there was one thing he loathed, it was rain on race day. Hopefully, it would pass before the driving sessions began or it would be another layer of unbearable stress on an already awful weekend.

He glared around as he entered the garage. 'Where's Lily?'

'Lily the mechanic?' Shane glanced up.

Massimo's glare hardened. How many Lilys were there?

Shane cleared his throat. 'She's on the track.'

'What?' He froze.

'In the display coupe.' Shane moved closer. 'Doing a track tour with a client.'

Massimo swivelled and registered the slick street, the lowered visibility. It was basically a monsoon out there.

'Are you telling me Lily Jones is driving on the circuit?' Massimo's voice rose to thunderous volumes. 'In one of our sports cars?'

'It's not a hot lap. She's not going all that fast.'

Oh he was wrong. Hearnshawe's top roadster had the

highest specs allowed for legal road use. It was far *too* fast. Why the hell had she agreed to get into it in her condition? After her ill health yesterday? In this *weather*?

'Bring her in now,' he snapped.

'But—'

'She ends the lap. Now. Slowly.'

'There's no headset.'

'Then get the fucking red flag!' Massimo stormed into the pit lane, leaving the man gaping.

He stood out in the lane, watching for the car to turn in, horrified at the rain bucketing down. It took too many seconds for her to appear. She braked, hitting the marks perfectly, coming to a stop right beside him despite the reduced visibility. Not that he could appreciate that. The hosing rain drowned his capacity to think. He could only act. Temper flaring, he jerked the driver's door open as she spoke to the passenger.

'I hope you enj—'

She broke off as he reached in and unfastened her seatbelt and grabbed her hand to help her out. He needed to make sure she was safe.

'What the hell are you doing?' he growled as soon as she was out of the car.

'What am *I* doing—what are *you* doing?' She sharply jerked her head.

He glanced back briefly and saw the pit crew behind him. They ought to be practising tyre changes; instead, they were gaping. Right. People. Honestly, he didn't care. All that had mattered was getting her out of the car in the rain. He would get that right this time.

As Shane moved forward to smooth things over with the startled passenger, Massimo glared at Lily.

'My office in the suites,' he muttered beneath his breath, conscious that she was now getting wet. 'Now.'

She stiffly marched through the garage ahead of him. His blasted phone rang. He irritably switched it to mute and shoved it back into his sodden pocket. Ahead of him Lily paused in the corridor. He stepped past, showing the way.

'What were you thinking?' She faced him as he closed the door and waved her hand in his direction. 'You're soaked through.'

He didn't give a damn. 'What was *I* thinking? You're the one driving too fast while pregnant!'

Her jaw dropped. 'It was a trundle around the track, not even at the normal speed limit.'

He couldn't contain the energy in his body. He'd nearly had a heart attack. 'You have huge things on your mind— you can't concentrate enough to drive safely.' It wasn't possible. He knew this. Emotions hindered clarity and performance.

'Of course I can,' she snapped. 'It *wasn't* fast. I didn't even need to wear a helmet.'

He stiffened. 'Is that meant to make me feel better?'

'You don't trust the safety features of your own car?' she asked.

'Not when it comes to you.'

'You're totally overreacting.'

'Look at the *rain*!' he roared.

She paused. He saw the moment she remembered. Of course she knew. Everyone fucking knew his parents had died in a high-speed car crash in the rain. But none of them knew *everything*. And he didn't want to see her *pity*. He was just too angry.

But he couldn't stop staring at her. Couldn't stop inhaling every damned aspect of her beauty. Water streamed down her lovely face, down her neck. Her sopping-wet top clung to every curve and straight of her body, revealing her tempting delicacy.

'You know I would never put my child at risk,' she said shakily. 'I can take care of myself.'

'Really? Have you even had breakfast?' He'd bet his fortune she hadn't. 'Why the hell are you—'

'Why are you here at all?' she interrupted fiercely. 'You don't usually come to the Singapore race!'

He blinked. He didn't come because he had a board meeting. One that, for the first time in five years, he'd rescheduled because he'd needed to see *her*. He was furious about his inability to resist being near her. And how did she even know? 'What makes you say that?'

Colour mottled her cheeks. She'd bothered to find out somehow. She'd been *pleased* to believe he wasn't going to be here. She didn't *want* him to be. So the pretty dress she'd worn last night hadn't been for him. Jealousy billowed through him in an outrageous, unstoppable wave.

'You can't be this controlling.' She furiously glared at him—gold flecks sparkled around those huge dark pupils.

His fury tripled. He'd played it her way last night. He'd gone against every instinct and left her when she'd asked. He'd respected her wishes. Why could she not respect his? Why had she come to work so damned early when he'd told her not to and then driven in conditions like these? He had every right to be irate. Her repeated rejections of anything he said or offered aggravated him more. It wasn't arrogance to know most women would've immediately said yes to his proposal. It was simple maths. The more billions he had in the bank, the more they were interested.

Was she really not interested at all? Had her taunting invitation for him to seduce her been a ploy? No, that all-access pass hadn't been offered entirely in anger. She still wanted him and he would prove it. He was compelled by irresistible physical need and she was, too. He could *see* it now in her jagged breathing, in her tight little nipples tormenting him through that slippery shirt, in her blooming flush. With a smothered groan he slammed her against the door with his whole body and pressed his lips to hers. *Hard.*

For a second she was completely still, then she ignited—*incandescent*—with anger. All fiery energy, she flung her arms around his neck and pressed just as hard back. Her lips parted and he stroked deep, but she curled her tongue, too, duelling with him over who claimed who. Fury kissing. He'd never known it before, never wanted it to end now. Her hands swept through his wet hair, her fingers tightening, twisting, holding him close to her with passionate anger. He felt her shudder, then her energy coil. She jumped the second he knew she would and he caught her, clutching her closer and higher so she wrapped her legs around his hips in an echo of those intimate moments in the air. Having her back in his hold—open and giving, *taking*—was everything. He lost his head. He would strip her, see her, have her. He wanted to take her entirely into him, to inhale her as if she were everything and all he needed to survive another second. He was filled with her heat and energy, feeling her beauty, her lush generosity. *This* was what he remembered. What he'd dreamt of night after night for the past two damned endless, agonising months. He'd ached for the way she flared with this exquisite responsiveness—she almost killed him with her fire. But slowly, the intensity between them altered. Anger lessened. Desire deepened.

He kissed down her neck, desperate to go lower, to lick and suck her breasts, to tease over her stomach and lower still. To have her utterly naked and his. But he was too busy drowning in the fiery demand of her kisses, her clutching limbs, to even start. Her moan destroyed him and he pressed her harder against the door, revelling in her supple, strong, silken body. The noises took a moment to impinge on his searing brain. She stilled the second he did. He lifted his lips from her and looked into her dazed, gleaming eyes—listening to the voices in the corridor but not hearing a word being said.

Shock chased the slumberous heat from her expression. He tried to relax his hold on her enough to lower her back to her feet but they were inches away from the satisfaction they both craved, and he almost couldn't let her go. Slowing his breathing hurt. Settling the searing ache in his body hurt more. He felt her shiver uncontrollably—a preamble to the orgasm now too far from her grasp and it was nothing but torture.

'You need to come back to the hotel,' he growled.

She leaned against the door and a fresh flush covered her face. Not lust this time; it was shame. He hated it.

'I told you it wouldn't make any difference,' she said.

He'd not kissed her to convince her to agree to anything monumental. He'd just wanted her. He'd needed to feel her strength and vitality.

'I need to concentrate on work.' She pulled her wet polo shirt away from her.

He just wanted to rip it right off her. 'You can't work this weekend.'

'Don't dictate.' Her eyes flashed.

He clenched his jaw.

'I'm not abandoning my team. It's not a home race. They can't just call up a replacement all that easily. I'm *fine* to keep working.' She looked at him accusingly. 'Until you have the results of the paternity test we've not even done, you can't have any influence over me whatsoever.'

'I know what the result will be. I know there hasn't been anyone since me.'

'How do you know that?' Colour swarmed into her cheeks all over again. 'Have you been spying on me somehow? Spent the night trying to dig up dirt?'

'Am I wrong?' He spread his hands around her waist, almost amused by her transparency, and knew he was not wrong. He could feel her trembling, see the embarrassment in her eyes, and the vulnerability tugged the truth from him. 'You're the only woman I've slept with in ages. Like you, I'm a workaholic and I like it that way.'

Her hazel eyes widened but her flush receded, leaving her too pale again. She was so delicately pretty.

'What about that princess?' she mumbled.

'Who?' He frowned, not comprehending.

'That princess in Belgium.'

His brain ticked slowly. Celine. The garage tour. 'You thought? Oh.' He suppressed his chuckle when he saw her spark. 'No. *No.*'

She stared into his face—assessing and untrusting.

'It's up to you whether or not you believe me,' he added

softly. 'But I promise I've not slept with anyone since you. There wasn't anyone for a while before you, either.'

Her anger—jealousy—was quite on display and helped ease the last of his tension from seeing her out there in that damned rain. They might have problems, but they definitely had chemistry, too. Maybe it would help them get through this initial upheaval.

Her teeth pressed on her lower lip. 'When we get back to England, we have the test done. Meanwhile, we get through the weekend. No one needs to know anything different.'

She was absurdly bothered about people knowing things. Unfortunately, he'd just hauled her off the track in front of everyone. He'd not gotten to where he was by waiting around for opportunities to reveal themselves. He went after them. He made them happen. He needed to move swiftly before the troubles deepened now. 'We need to make arrangements sooner than that.'

'*After* the race,' she said. 'I might be one of fifty mechanics and not the singular oh-so-important CEO of everything, but my *work* matters to me. Don't stop me from it. It's all I have.'

All? He stilled. She really knew how to make him feel like a bastard. What had happened to make work everything in her life? What had she *lost* for it to have become so all consuming? Because in his very personal experience, an imbalance like this was a result of something missing.

He watched her, knowing it was going to take a while to work out, but he had the resources to restore whatever it was she now lacked. She wouldn't suffer more because of this. Which is why they needed to take the time to talk this through. But she was never going to respond well to him railroading her.

'Okay,' he conceded. 'Work this weekend but the second the race is over, we talk.'

He would make some arrangements regardless. Having her in his arms again cemented his decision. He'd never wanted a family, he'd never been worthy of a family, but this had happened and honour still mattered.

She nodded. 'Meanwhile, we keep this quiet.'

That was going to be impossible. 'There's no keeping this a secret for long.' He lightly stroked his palm over her lower belly, unable to resist touching her again. 'You're so tiny. It'll be no time before you start showing.'

He could hardly bear to think of her blooming with their child. It terrified him all over again.

'Thanks for making me feel self-conscious,' she murmured, her breathing quickening beneath his hand.

'Is that what I make you feel?' He bent closer, drawn by those brown and green and gold flecks, and brushed his lips over hers. With that irresistible stolen touch, he let the secret slip. 'You scared the hell out of me, Lily. Don't do it again.'

CHAPTER SEVEN

Message if you need anything.

As. If. Lily was inexplicably angry at the offer. Massimo was being chivalrous but not with the intention she wanted; this was *duty* not genuine desire. So she didn't reply. Though she did reread the text every ten minutes. He was being polite, probably trying to keep tabs, but no one ever asked if she needed anything, and that he had was touching. She scoffed at herself. It would serve him right if she sent back a twenty-line list of cravings. Except she had only *one*.

Friday's practice sessions passed in a blur of speed, sound and stress. The heat was fierce, the crowds vast, DJs kept a pulsing beat for stilt-walkers and sword-swallowers, creating a festival atmosphere that Lily would've adored if she weren't so distracted by the spectacular crash in her personal life. Yet, instead of focusing on the really big issue—the baby—she spent ages wondering whether to believe that she really was the only woman he'd slept with recently. She wanted to believe him. In her world, the chemistry between them wasn't normal. But she couldn't be sure.

Her body signals were scrambled. That fiery moment

yesterday had overwhelmed her and she craved more because it was unfinished, that was all.

Now there were looks. Definitely whispers. Gossip swirled faster in the paddock than the cars did on track. She'd disappeared into the CEO's office for ten minutes yesterday and it was nothing short of scandalous. Part of her didn't care—the same part that could only recall the sight of him in there. His tailored white shirt was gorgeous enough but soaked to the skin, it was raw fuel igniting her engine. She'd not *seen* him on the cargo plane; now she wanted nothing more than to see *all* of him. But it had been so long since she'd enjoyed *any* physical contact—so even the lightest amount, the simplest touch of his hand, set her off. It was only the fraught situation—the uncertainty and speed of it—heightening her feelings. So they were unreliable, right? She focused on her routine checks to stop herself ruminating. Work was the only thing she could truly rely on.

'You okay, Lily?' Shane said softly. 'Need backup?'

'Thank you.' She smiled, but then saw the curiosity in Shane's eyes. With her ability to trust her instincts long destroyed, she couldn't decide if he was prying or being protective. She opted for gentle defence. 'But I can handle the heat as well as anyone.'

Chocolate almonds? Cherries? No request too small. Anything. Anytime.

Details this time. Personal, teasing ones. Another message she definitely couldn't answer.

On Saturday night they held the qualifying session to determine the starting order for Sunday's race. The atmosphere was oppressive and rain was forecast. Lily felt wiped out by the stifling humidity; honestly, she would welcome the rain if qualification wasn't starting soon.

'Do you think it's going to be bad enough for inters or will we get away with slicks for the session?'

She glanced up. Emiliano was leaning beside the wall, watching her prep the tyres. Every other time he'd talked to her she'd answered briefly before moving away, but today she welcomed the distraction. There was already talk behind her back; more now wouldn't matter. Especially not when they found out what was really going on.

'We'll have all options available,' she answered. 'The track temperature might have the greater impact than rain. Depending.' There were always so many variables.

'Because it's street?'

'Yes, it's rougher. That's going to affect the wear.'

They discussed street versus purpose-built track surfaces versus heavy rain for a solid ten minutes before he was called to the strategy room. Lily appreciated the reprieve from her own thoughts—she could talk tyres all day.

As qualifying began, every grandstand around the track was filled. The energetic crowd was almost loud enough to drown the scream of engines pushed to their limits. The threat of rain increased the urgency to get the session done before it hit. Both Conrad and Emiliano had made it through to the top ten but in the closing minutes of qualifying, the skies opened and the rain tumbled. Visibility was instantly reduced; slipperiness increased. Everyone stilled in the pit, focused on the screens—watching the cars cling on through their final lap. The downpour was heavy. Would the race stewards be debating suspending the session so close to the finish?

Lily glanced to the side as she caught a movement out of the corner of her eye. Massimo had appeared in the small section of the garage where VIP guests watched. She was stunned. He *never* watched in public but now he was here, headset on to listen to team radio, rigidly staring at the screens.

Lily wanted to watch Massimo as much as the last qualifying lap. *Not okay.* Not when it was late and hot and wet and more focus than ever was required. Even though right now hers was all on Conrad and Emiliano handling the cars they were in. Her nerves shredded, she felt ill with the increasing hazards as the rain fell in sheets. At the fourth corner, Conrad spun but managed to stay on track long enough to veer into the overshoot lane. With no red flag, Emiliano sent it into the last corner and in the final seconds pushed his time to the top of the field. The roar in the garage was instant and deafening as the mechanics around her cheered and clapped. Emiliano had secured his first pole position—he'd be starting tomorrow's race at the front of all the others. She dare not turn to see Massimo's reaction.

'You were right about the track!' Emiliano shouted to her as he was swamped by the mechanics when he got back to the garage.

She'd not said anything the strategists wouldn't have said. She'd just called it before he'd had the chance to talk to them, but she was quietly thrilled to have been right. Turning, she caught Massimo's gaze. Despite Emiliano's success he couldn't seem to smile. Of course he couldn't. She was pregnant and a wholly unsuitable partner for him.

Moments later he walked out and took her vitality with him.

Just ask. I dare you.

The message pinged first thing on race day. She ignored it. She didn't ask anyone for anything. She took care of things herself and if she really had to get someone's help—like she had Derek's—then she made sure she took only the minimum necessary and then paid them back. She would owe no one anything. She would rely only on herself. But as she lay in bed, she knew she couldn't work the race tonight. She was too distracted. Too tired. She would make a mistake and she never wanted to be the one who lost them any advantage. It was terrible to let them down, but the fact was she had to resign anyway.

Soon enough she wouldn't be able to travel. She'd be enormously pregnant, not even allowed on a plane. She needed a new plan, to switch up her life completely. She would leave the racing circuit and get a job at a general garage, focus on cam belts and gear boxes. Maybe once the baby was born she could go back part-time. She would make it work. But the awful thing was she was going to need some help.

In the afternoon she dragged herself to the track but Shane came over and spoke before she could admit she had to let him down.

'You're not needed in the garage tonight,' he said. 'Go watch from the grandstand. Enjoy it.'

She looked up at him a little sadly. There were no rest days in P1, certainly not on race days. 'Is this a request from management?'

'No,' he said quietly. 'We both know you're not one hundred percent. Come back fully refreshed after the break.'

'Thanks, Shane.' She hesitated then looked at him directly. 'I'm really sorry.'

She didn't have the heart to tell him she wasn't likely to be returning at all.

In the change room she slipped out of her uniform and into a loose summer dress. She hadn't the right to wear the team gear; she was a failure. A *fraud*. She wouldn't stay in the paddock with the VIPs and celebrities. She would go into the main spectator area and watch the race alongside thousands of passionate, ordinary fans. She would message Massimo in the morning. Deal with everything after the race as they'd agreed. But she'd only made it a few hundred metres into the fan zone when a heavy arm landed across her shoulders.

'Going somewhere?'

Lily stopped. His hand squeezed. He had a cap tugged very low and she couldn't believe she'd been such a blind fool on that cargo plane. His dazzling cornflower-blue eyes were so unique.

'How did you know where I was?'

He jerked his chin to her left.

She followed his glance and saw the tall man a few feet from her. 'You put security on me?'

'For protection, not imprisonment,' he murmured dryly. 'Keep walking. We wouldn't want to create *drama*.'

He was mocking her, but at the same time had a point. He would be recognised any second.

'I wasn't going to *leave*,' she muttered. 'I was just going to look around.'

'I'll go with you. This way.'

There were so many people around them it was impossible not to move in the direction he was guiding her. She realised the tall guy to her left wasn't the only bodyguard. There were four of them barely blending in as they carved their way through the crowd.

'I'm not needed in the garage for the race. I'm free to spectate.' She couldn't keep the bitterness out of her voice.

'We'll watch it together.'

But he led her *behind* the main grandstands, to the waterfront. She knew some VIPs arrived at the circuit via boat. She'd seen the beautiful launches crossing the harbour, taking them from their luxury hotels to the elite spectator suites. So she wasn't all that surprised when Massimo took her to a gleaming wooden boat waiting at the jetty.

Lily didn't bother trying to argue; she just stepped on board with a sense of fatalism. The immaculately poised stewards didn't blink at the sight of her flushed, overheated self and the bodyguards fell back. Lily sat at the rear; she hadn't the strength to resist Massimo's wishes. They needed to talk; this needed to be sorted. Yet, she felt a pang as they pulled away from the vibrant noise.

'You shouldn't miss the race,' she finally spoke.

She'd not missed one since starting with Hearnshawe.

'I prefer to watch in private anyway.'

He'd not said it suggestively yet temptation smoked through her. She gritted her teeth. So much for thinking she'd be better off not working. She needed more focus than ever just to stay sane around Massimo.

It took only minutes to cross the water and dock at the

hotel. With an elegant sweep of his arm, he helped her to disembark. His courtesy made her discomfort prickle.

They went straight into a gleaming elevator and were whisked quickly to the sky. The doors slid open to reveal an enormous suite. Lily moved to the large windows to take in the fascinating skyline—so many skyscrapers, brilliant, unique feats of architecture. She heard Massimo murmuring and glanced back to see him welcoming room service in. She watched them unload a trolley onto the gleaming dining table with amazement. He must've ordered it while they were on the boat. Dumplings, skewered meats, vibrant salad and a colourful array of sliced fruit. All tempting, nibblish things.

'Come and eat.' Massimo pulled a chair out for her as soon as they were alone again.

She shook her head as she sat. 'You don't have to—'

'Be polite?' he mocked gently.

'You weren't like this on the plane. Don't change just because the circumstances have.'

'Actually, I was like this. I fed you chocolate almonds and let you lean on my shoulder.'

She squeezed her hands into fists, quelling the desire to throttle him. 'I shouldn't have done that.'

'It's okay to lean on someone—'

'Do *you* do that often?' She glanced up and challenged directly.

Why should she be more dependent than he?

'Sure, I have very good staff who help me.'

Staff wasn't quite what she'd meant. But of course, like her, he had minimal family. He didn't have any particularly *personal* support and it seemed he didn't want it. He kept his distance from everyone, even Emiliano. The kid had an entourage of experts around him but Massimo wasn't generally in it. So why on earth would he want to push them both into *marriage*?

She couldn't reconcile the man who'd easily slipped into warm humour and intimacy on the cargo plane, with this one who was so damned bossy and rigidly determined.

'Everything is going to be okay, Lily.'

She picked up a dumpling, saving herself from having to answer; plus, it gave her something to do with her hands and mouth—because she really wanted to feast on him. Yeah, there was still that problem to be dealt with. He, too, tucked in as if he'd not eaten in days. In time, they demolished almost everything. And then she needed a different distraction so she didn't have to look into his spellbinding eyes.

'Shouldn't we watch the race?' She nodded towards the large screen.

It would be underway now.

'There'll be plenty of other races to watch when we're married.'

Heat frothed in her blood. 'We're not—' She broke off and inhaled deeply. 'You *can't* be serious about that.'

'I don't joke about life-changing decisions.' He cocked his head. 'Am I really so unpalatable? Am I the worst man in the world? Or is it that I'm not ordinary enough?'

The bitter edge beneath his light mockery sharpened her senses.

'That's right,' she said. 'You're nowhere *near* normal enough for a simple girl like me.'

'You're not simple, Lily. Nor are you ordinary.'

'Flattery won't work.'

'It might not be so awful. I can give you an amazing lifestyle.'

'I thought I wasn't getting millions to live the high life,' she muttered dryly. 'For the record I've never wanted to be a kept woman, nor do I want my child to become so spoilt he expects to get his own way all the time.'

Massimo's smile was slow and appreciative. 'Are you suggesting I'm spoilt?'

She stiffened, trying to stop her heated reaction to that smile. 'Are you suggesting you aren't?'

'You like to be spoilt, too. You like the occasional cherry on top.'

She'd taken the *one* once, and look where it had gotten her.

'Marry me and I'll spoil you in ways you've never even imagined,' he coaxed.

That dreadfully inappropriate heat washed over her. He wasn't talking about sex. Or at least he shouldn't be.

'As tempting as that offer undoubtedly is, I'm afraid I'm going to have to pass.'

His smile remained steady. 'Why are you so determined to reject me?'

'It's for your own good,' she said, time to be serious. 'I told you I'm not from a suitable background.'

'You mean because you don't come from money?'

'I mean my kind never marries your kind.' She nodded. 'You're so posh you're practically royalty. You're certainly *racing* royalty. You hang out with actual princesses. If you go public with me, it'll impact your business. Your bottom line.'

'Golly.' He leaned back, blue eyes twinkling. 'What's

wrong with your *kind*? You said you grew up in a garage—that's my family business, too.'

'That's one part of my family business,' she snapped coldly. 'It's also a chop shop. My father flips stolen car parts and my mother cooks the books.'

He blinked. 'Okay but—'

'I have two older brothers. One is dead. The other is in jail and it's my fault he's there.'

He fell silent, finally serious. Good.

'It *is* a family business.' She made herself tell him everything. It would end his *must marry* madness. 'My father's the boss. He issues the orders, we obey. Everyone has their job. Mine was on reception. I always wanted to work on the cars but he said I was too small, but I watched and learned anyway. I would work with my brothers when our parents were at the pub. I was fast.'

'I'm sure. I've seen you in action.'

'And I was a swot. Not just in the garage, but at school. I thought I'd get their approval, but all I got was too good at maths for Mum to let me see the accounts.'

'You knew what she was doing?'

'It wasn't hard to work out. As I got older, I watched my brothers take more and more risks. Stealing cars, modifying them for illegal street races. Dad encouraged them. He wanted good parts. But while Callum liked a fast car, he didn't always want to put the work in. He rushed repairs in order to race more. If he'd just slowed down then it might've been okay. But one night he'd rushed it too much. Finn was driving...' She paused, steadied herself. He needed to know. 'They'd barely left the garage when I heard the impact. They were both flung from the car.

Callum was killed instantly. Finn was charged with dangerous driving.'

She paused again. Massimo was regarding her intently, his expression inscrutable. He'd never discussed the accident that had killed his parents and she wondered again about the scars up his forearm.

'The thing is, Finn had already been convicted for car theft and with this he faced jail time. My parents told me to say I'd seen Callum driving, not Finn. That the lie would save Finn from jail.'

The accident and the aftermath in her final year of school had changed everything.

'I couldn't do it,' she whispered. 'I was in shock about Callum. I knew Finn would race again and I didn't want him to. I wanted him to stay safe, stay alive. But they never forgave me for not doing as they said.'

'They never should have asked you to lie,' Massimo said quietly, his focus steady on her. 'The authorities would have found out the truth—surely there would have been evidence showing what really happened. Saying that would've only gotten you into trouble and negatively impacted your future.'

Which was also partly why she'd refused. She'd had ambition bigger than the family business. 'Right. As they said, I was too selfish to put the family first.'

'Was it really *family* first?' His eyes narrowed. 'Or was it your *brother* before you? Again?'

She failed to answer. He was too astute. Her dreams had never been given any consideration. It had been about her father, her brother; she'd just been expected to fall in.

'What happened then?' Massimo softly pressed.

'They threw me out.' Banished and branded her a traitor. She'd lost her community, too. Her boyfriend—her brother's friend—had never spoken to her again. She'd been utterly cut.

'What about your mother? Didn't she stick up for you?'

Her mother never stood up to her father, never stood up for Lily. Lily would never do that to *her* child. She would hold her baby close and protect it from every kind of pressure.

'How old were you?' Massimo breathed.

'Seventeen.'

Anger flashed in his eyes. 'Did you finish school? Where did you *live*?'

'I stole some cash on my way out,' she admitted. She was filled with shame about that, but she'd had no choice. She'd had a couple of bad nights. Doors slammed in her face because her family had spread the word not to welcome her. Their rejection had been so cruel, so complete. 'I was so at a loss, in the end I got on a bus and went to the track. I'd never been before. I just used to watch it on screen, you know? But it had always been the dream to get there. I hung around and asked for odd jobs every day until Derek gave me a chance. When he saw what I could do, he helped me find an apprenticeship at a local garage. I worked the junior karting leagues after hours and on the weekends.'

She'd worked every hour she could, made connections in the field. She was proud of her efforts and immeasurably grateful to the old guy for supporting her.

Massimo's frown had deepened. 'Your parents didn't want to lose another son, so they threw away their daughter.'

She flinched. He was right, but to hear it put so succinctly was like a punch.

'I'm sorry—' He broke off and swore. 'But your brother, parents, friends, home, school, you lost everything. I'm sorry your brother died. I get they were grieving, but they shouldn't have done that to you—'

'But they did and I'm better off without them in my life.'

'You're not in touch with them at all?' he asked. 'Your brother?'

'I've sent care packages to him but had no reply.'

'Lily…'

A hard lump formed in her throat and she couldn't look up. She didn't want to allow his anger to soothe her. She didn't want to revisit the wounds that she'd worked hard to hide, but were still raw. She hadn't told him to get his sympathy. He simply needed to understand why he had to keep his distance. 'They think I'm disloyal and when they find out about you, they'll strike. They'll ask for things.' They were greedy and entitled in a different way to him, in a worse way. 'They'll damage you, Massimo. They'll cause gossip and scandal and—'

'You don't need to worry about me. I can handle them.' He put his hand over hers. '*You* don't want everything in your life exposed. It still hurts.'

Of course it still hurt.

'Rejection *always* hurts,' she said roughly. 'Especially when it's people who are supposed to love you.'

The pain of their rejection—that absolute ostracism—wasn't something she'd ever allow to happen to her again.

'But *I'm* okay.' She didn't want him pitying her. 'And I had support. Derek and Jean were incredible. They let me live in the caravan at the edge of their property the whole time I was an apprentice. I—'

'A caravan?' he interrupted, incredulous. 'Not their house?'

'I didn't want that,' she said stiffly.

He had no right to judge them; that had been her choice. She was never going to invade the older couple's space. They'd been more than generous enough to her.

'I needed my independence and the caravan was wonderful,' she said defensively. 'It's cosy and safe and I can heat it in minutes. I have everything I need in the one room.'

'You still live there?' His incredulity didn't lessen.

'While I'm in the travelling crew. I like going back there. They don't charge me nearly enough rent. I still owe them.'

She'd never wanted to overstep—she'd needed help but tried to take as little as possible and paid back in volunteer hours at the track.

'I'll take care of it,' he said.

'No, it's *my* debt,' she said huskily. 'I wouldn't have told you if I'd thought you'd do that. That's *not* what I want—'

'But it's what can happen.' His nostrils flared. 'What *should* happen.'

'Because you've gotten me pregnant?' She shook her head. He didn't need to assume entire responsibility for her life's failures. She didn't need rescuing and she didn't want to cause him more problems than he'd ever intended to take on. 'You're missing the point. We *can't* marry. You can't have in-laws who—'

'Sound like they're not going to impact on us, given they have nothing to do with you,' he interrupted bluntly.

She winced. 'But they'll try. And people will find out. They'll probably try to sell secrets they don't even know. And all your precious sponsors, all those brand collaborations with the drivers. No one will *trust* you if you're with me. They're small time but they're still scandalous. They'll tarnish your reputation.'

'Wealthy people can weather all kinds of controversies. We get away with almost anything,' he said quietly. 'A few criminal elements is nothing. Every family has them. Half the wealthy are dodgy, you know.'

'Not like this.' She shook her head. 'You care too much about your company to let any connection with me wreck it.'

He smiled. 'If you're that worried, we'll get the social media team to soft launch us. It'll be fine.'

Soft launch? 'You mean we'll be a PR strategy?' She was utterly offended. 'So I'm like a product? Do I need personal branding? I'm not going to be a commodity you're going to sell to the public.'

Would the baby be another product eventually?

So. Not. Fine.

'Maybe our marriage will attract attention, but many aspects of my life are kept completely private. Ultimately, our relationship will be as well,' he said. 'Suitability isn't a reason to say no. You're just trying to find excuses because you're scared and I get that. This is unexpected and overwhelming but you can trust me.'

She stared at him, speechless. She *couldn't*. She couldn't count on anyone other than herself. And how could he not see how completely wrong of a fit she would be in his life?

'We should watch the race.' She pushed away from the table, drawn towards the windows. The sky had darkened; now those buildings were even more spectacular and she could see the extra bright lights of the track. Far below them the water moved gently in a dark, sultry celebration. It was truly beautiful.

'Emiliano is on pole,' she said. 'He might make his first podium.'

'I'll find out later—'

'He's your cousin.'

'You're my future wife.'

'Don't, Massimo.'

His whispered promise of priority hit her weakest spot. But independence was her absolute bedrock and she couldn't concede it. Even when he looked at her like this—so intense, so *hot*.

'Lily.' He moved to stand right in front of her. His breathing was ragged and his hands were flexed into fists the same way hers were. 'Do you think we could pause the argument for a while? Neither of us are at our best.'

She could laugh and cry at the same time. 'Are you not?'

Because he looked it to her.

'I'm hopelessly distracted,' he confessed.

'By the race?'

'Not the race, no.'

He was close enough for her to sense his heat, for her to be unable to see anything beyond his taut, muscled body.

His blue eyes burned into her. 'Do I still have the

access-all-areas pass you so generously flung at me the other night?'

Her blood fizzed, smothering every concern in an instant.

'We have an issue between us, Lily, and I don't mean the baby.'

No, he meant this inexorable pull, stronger than gravity, as undeniable as the need to breathe. 'Do you think we should deal with the issue and then discuss the serious matters?'

'Exactly.'

She should be sensible. She should stop and think. But she didn't. Instead, she flung herself over the edge. *Yes.*

But he didn't sweep her into his arms, didn't kiss her with the intense, furious abandon of yesterday. No, now he was slow and deliberate and so very vexing.

'Massimo…'

His hands were light, gentle, slow, carefully sliding the thin straps from her shoulders. With the curtains open, the room received enough light from that vibrant neon skyline—more than enough for her to see his expression, and that was more than enough to keep her still. To savour this.

'I've dreamed of seeing you,' he muttered. 'Finally, I get to see *all* of you.'

The dress pooled at her feet and he stared. 'You're stunning.' He looked in her eyes and smiled. 'You don't believe me?' He moved faster to shed his own clothes, unashamedly stepping out of his trousers. 'Look at what you do to me.'

Oh she was looking. She was inhaling his long limbs,

the strong muscles. Her mouth dried. Finally naked and he was everything. Drop-dead gorgeous. She began to shake.

In a flurry of movement so fast it was a blur, they both stepped forward. In less than a blink they were *together*. It was frantic. She didn't just say yes, she surrendered completely. They were both unleashed, all control gone and thus in an instant it was impossibly intimate. Instinct—touch and taste—was everything. She was kindling, a roaring fire in seconds and unable to be contained. He tried. He lifted her and carried her to the bed, not bothering with curtains nor light, just letting that skyline illuminate her skin. There was nowhere to hide but she was too hot to feel self-conscious, too lost to this indulgence, too joyous in her exploration of *him*.

'Breathe.' He kissed down her body, tearing her underwear in his frantic haste. *'Breathe.'*

She'd not realised she wasn't and she didn't care anyway; she just needed to touch him.

'Slow down,' he muttered as she rose above him. 'Slow down.'

'I can't.' She needed to be with him. It couldn't happen fast enough.

'We have all night,' he half laughed.

And that wasn't going to be long enough. She arched, grinding against him until he flipped and pinned her. She moaned as he grazed his teeth along her inner thigh before fastening his mouth on her, his tongue rasping in rough but gentle strokes. Her bones liquefied. Her very soul melted. She'd missed this so much and she desperately wanted more. Never had she wanted anything as much as she wanted this. *'Please!'*

But the orgasm screamed through her before she could stop it.

His triumphant laugh was further erotic torment as it gusted over her lower belly. As soon as she could, she arched beneath him. This was no dance, but a battle. With a groan he braced above her, staring into her eyes for ever so slightly too long.

'Massimo,' she whispered. She pleaded.

He gave in, thrusting hard and deep, pushing all his strength into her. She gasped, relishing his complete claim.

'Yes.' She bucked up to meet him.

'I like hearing that word on your lips,' he growled, flexing harder into her.

'You'll only get it here. Doing this.'

His smile was feral, his body fast. Another orgasm hurtled upon her. Too much. Too soon. *All* too soon. She closed her eyes and wrapped her limbs tightly around him, trying to hang on as long and as hard as she could, but all too soon she was lost over the edge. And to her infinite satisfaction, he tumbled with her.

She couldn't open her eyes, but in the distance she heard the booms and sparks from the end of race celebrations across the bay.

'I think we missed the fireworks,' she murmured brokenly.

'*You're* the fireworks,' he chuckled. 'I need a flame-proof suit but it's worth being burned by you.'

Indeed, she was burning up. He'd worked her over—ruthlessly, relentlessly, *generously*. But she was greedy for his intensity, his determination, his strength. He had more of those things than anyone she'd ever met. More than *she* had.

'There's one thing you need to understand, Lily.' He moved, using his body to cage her beneath him.

'Mmm?'

'I'm not the cherry on top. I'm the whole damn cake. And the only one you're enjoying for the foreseeable future. Understood?'

CHAPTER EIGHT

'DID YOU SLEEP WELL?' Massimo watched her approach.

She still looked sleepy with slight smudges beneath her dazed eyes; her skin was flushed and a streak of stubble rash marked her neck. She looked like she'd spent half the night being thoroughly pleasured. Which she had. All Massimo wanted now was to take her back to bed and carry on. But she tightly fastened the hotel robe around her slim body, hiding her dreamy curves. Manhandling her the second she was conscious wasn't the calm-and-in-control aura he ought to exude.

'You know I did.' She ran a hand through her hair, the long waves tempting him more. 'Eventually.'

Yeah, it had been a wrench to leave her there. He'd woken only an hour ago, his brain whirring. He'd investigated—read the local news articles about her brothers' accident and the few other mentions of her family. Her fear that they would negatively impact him was unfounded. He had a solution. Money talked and he had plenty of it. People did turn a blind eye when you could pay for almost anything and he was happy to pay for their compliance, but he was furious they'd abandoned a teenager who should have been valued and protected, not used and threatened.

She took in the fact that he was fully dressed and clutched her robe closer about her. 'I should get moving.'

'Yes,' he agreed peaceably. 'Your bag has already been collected from the other hotel. The team has completed the pack-out and they're in the air already.' He leaned in to his controlling self. 'We're going to Sentosa for a few days. Beach holiday.'

Her face was a picture. 'You can't just—'

'Did you have other plans for the break? A trip booked?' he interrupted blandly. 'Or were you just going back to the caravan?'

She shot him a reproachful look.

'I know. Too high-handed.' He grinned. But a long flight now—even by private jet—was too much for her. 'We need to work things through. You need privacy and rest. You look wiped out.'

'Thanks,' she said sarcastically.

He wasn't about to apologise; it was true. And no wonder when she'd been so isolated for so long. Her prickliness, her determined independence, now made sense. Abandoned by her family, she'd lost trust and developed a ferocious need for independence as defence. Aside from simply needing to survive, when her own family didn't value her, how did she find value within herself? Through work.

He knew the drill. He'd tried that himself. But where she'd succeeded, he'd failed. Because she was fundamentally worthy, whereas he was not.

He wished she would just be shallow and say yes to everything—not just this trip, but to marrying him. Why couldn't she simply accept the lifestyle he could offer? She and the baby could be secure within the Hearnshawe gates. He would set her up with everything she needed, just as he'd done for Emiliano. Only she didn't seem to want that so now he felt forced to try to convince her—to *prove* why it could work. He feared she wanted more than what his money could buy. That she wanted the things he didn't and would never have. It was too bad, because the die was cast and the sooner they settled into it, the better.

'Honestly, I need a break, too,' he added huskily. He actually bloody did. He was damned tired.

She studied him searchingly, no doubt seeing the shadows beneath his eyes; plus, he'd not yet bothered to shave. Seeing that abrasion on her neck, he would in a moment. For now he waited, enduring her scrutiny until at last she nodded.

He smiled ruefully. Of course she was more comfortable with the idea if she thought *he* got some benefit as well. Then it wasn't all about her. Was she so used to not being considered that she almost felt threatened when she was?

'What will you have for breakfast?' he asked.

'Umm...' She glanced sideways at the tray at the end of the table, her nose wrinkled. 'Actually, do you think it's possible for me to see a doctor? Not because there's anything wrong—but just have a check-up, make sure my nutrition is everything it should be. That sort of thing.'

'Of course.' It was already on his list, but that she'd raised it first was good. She'd not replied to his texts through the weekend, but she needed to learn that when she did ask, he would deliver. Starting now. 'I'll arrange for one to come to the hotel in Sentosa. We'll leave as soon as you've dressed.'

'Amazing, thank you.'

He grabbed his phone to message instructions while she went hunting for her dress. Within a half hour the car arrived.

'Don't you want to drive?' she murmured.

'Not when I can be in the back seat with you.' He winked.

'But you raced for a while. You won several of the karting grades year on year in England. Why did you stop?'

He quelled his discomfort. He couldn't tell her what had happened the last day he'd gone racing. 'I needed to concentrate on my education. After my father died, I knew I would take over Hearnshawe sooner and I needed the skills to succeed.'

'Surely, driving is one of those skills.'

'I knew all I needed to. There were other areas I had to focus on.' He was relieved when they arrived at the hotel.

He watched an element of panic enter her wide eyes as she walked into their private villa.

'This place is amazing,' she murmured.

The villa was lovely but Massimo's home on the edge of an Italian lake had more space. He would take her there later. He didn't want to overwhelm her too soon—she was skittish enough of how *spoilt* he was. Her expectations were shockingly low. She liked the cosiness of a damned cramped caravan. A gradual introduction to his world would definitely be best. Plus, in this neutral space, she couldn't hide from him.

'It must cost—'

'Don't.' He leaned against the wall. 'You know you can withdraw my all-access pass again at any time. Or not. This isn't a transaction. People sometimes do things for each other without expecting or demanding something in return.'

'I can't give to you in the same way.'

'I don't want you to. You don't have to give me anything.' She didn't understand that just her smile gave him satisfaction.

'Just my hand in marriage,' she pointed out.

Oh yeah, there was that.

'I won't marry you, but I'm still going to say thank you,' she said proudly. 'I don't take this for granted. I know your time is precious.'

'No more precious than yours. Time is a complete leveller. Finite for everyone, and none of us knows how much we'll really have.' He scooped up her bag but she stepped in front of him.

'I can do that,' she said stiffly, trying to take it from him.

'I know,' he said, tightening his grip. 'But you don't have to.'

Her chin lifted. 'I can and do accept help. When I want to.'

'Sure,' he drawled. 'As little as possible.'

He flexed and finally she let go, let him put the damned bag in her room. Having things done for her definitely made her uncomfortable. He was offering only basic courtesy but she wasn't used to being treated well. She would become accustomed to staff supporting her. He'd watched her work her butt off over these past weeks. She was nimble, quick, on hand with the right tool with surgical precision. She always worked extra hours, always went the extra mile. She was focused, diligent, ruthlessly competent. She'd clawed her way into P1 because failure wasn't an option. This wasn't just desire; this was survival for her. But while she wanted to be part of the team, she kept slightly distanced. Head down, walls up. A defensive strategy he also used. And when she'd thought she was alone and away from the team, she'd indulged in a cherry—a rare tiny treat. No wonder she was hungry for touch. She should have so much more. He would ensure she did—in that arena at least, he could deliver.

'The doctor will be here after lunch,' he said when he got back to the lounge and found her sprawled on the sofa, enjoying the air-conditioned room.

'What are we going to do until then?' she murmured.

'Whatever we want.' Awareness rippled through him as he saw that gleam in her eyes.

A small smile curved her mouth. 'Shall we watch the race replay?'

'Sure.' He was not disappointed. He had patience.

He programmed the smart screen then sprawled beside her, muted his phone and flipped it face down to ignore the never-ending succession of calls and messages. Work could wait. He was spending just a little precious time with her. But the moment the music began, Lily was lost to him.

'Oh no.' She winced as she watched Emiliano lose the lead in the first lap. 'Oh that's such a shame.'

She was glued to the action and there was plenty of it, but Massimo barely paid attention to the screen; watching her was too entertaining. She was a bundle of nervous energy. Maybe this wasn't such a great idea; it was completely winding her up.

'Oh he's pitting.' She slid off the sofa to kneel on the rug, even closer to the screen.

'Why are you so keyed up when you already know the result?' He chuckled.

She held up a hand to silence him. 'Fast. That was good. They practice over and over.'

Yeah, he was aware, but she watched all the other team's pit stops with the same intensity. Calling out the strategy. Wincing when Conrad's car kissed the wall after an impressive overtake. Her energy was infectious—he sank into her sparkling excitement. He never wanted to watch another race without her beside him. Ever.

She watched as Conrad recovered places to get into third position, while Emiliano surged back to second. 'There's the moment!' she squealed.

He laughed. She glanced and caught him staring and suddenly turned red.

'I'm sorry,' she said. 'You should've been there to celebrate with him.'

'You should've been with the team. You worked hard to help them get that result.' His throat was parched and swallowing was tricky. 'But honestly, I have no regrets.'

It just slipped out, but he realised he truly didn't. He never missed watching a race—even when he wasn't actually at the event he watched it live online. But he'd missed it completely last night and he didn't give a damn. He didn't regret that night on the cargo plane, either. He could never regret any of the moments they'd shared.

She'd gone completely still, almost as if she were transfixed. Despite the air-conditioning, Massimo was suddenly sweltering and his chest tightened. His heart thundered, pumping hot blood everywhere—was she *blushing*?

He didn't know but suddenly she was. Again. A fresh

flush swept not just her cheeks, but her shoulders, her décolletage, and he sank into her sweet smile.

'Not interested in the race anymore?' He could hardly speak.

'I know what happens.'

His heart almost thumped right out of his chest as she suddenly crawled the short distance to arrive at his feet.

She looked up at him. 'Do I have an access-all-areas pass from you?'

'Absolutely.' Desire enveloped him as heat ignited those gold flecks in her eyes. 'What...?'

He broke off as she shook her head. Still not ready to talk? Nor was he in this moment. She rose to her knees and put her hands on his legs, pushing them farther apart. He allowed it—right now he would let her do whatever she wanted.

'You want to drive?' he muttered breathlessly.

'I want to *play*.'

His body melted as she moved closer. He ran his hand through her long, glossy hair and she shimmied, teasing it over his lap. She was wild and sweet and yes, so playful as she tormented him with long pulls of her small hands and deep sucks of her hot mouth. His head fell back as she did what she wanted with him. What he ached for. Shuddering, he closed his eyes, but it didn't protect him from the unfolding intimacy. This wasn't play; it was *personal*. So deeply, intensely, profoundly special. She took no mere taste of cake, but something far more substantial. Something dangerous. He groaned, shifting his hips, unable to bear it as all control slipped from him. He needed this to be less. Less intense. Less caring. Less sweet. But it was too late. He fisted his hands in her hair, unable to warn her any other way. But she didn't stop. No, she tightened her grip and sucked him deeper until he thrust too hard, groaning as he pulsed with furious bursts of euphoria.

He collapsed back, unable to move. It was only at her soft chuckle that he opened his eyes. She was still on her knees, looking directly up at him. Her dreamy, frankly smug expression energised him like a damned defibrillator. His muscles jerked and he swiftly reached forward, grasping her waist to lift her onto his lap. Her soft gasp turned him inside out.

'Aren't you out of gas?' she squeaked as she straddled him and realised that one part of him had roared right back to life.

He really should be. He swept his hands over her hips. 'Apparently, my engine is solar-powered and *you* are the sun.'

Her smile blossomed—unguarded and open and suddenly he was the triumphant one. He swept his hands beneath her dress, lifting it. She raised her arms and he whisked it off. He leaned close, kissing her creamy skin. She was so responsive. She didn't bother taking off her panties; she just knelt up enough to pull them to the side before sliding down on him hard and to the hilt.

'So hot,' he growled.

She was a dynamo. A petite passion bomb who unleashed a maelstrom of energy and emotion and infected him with the same. Her impact should never be underestimated. He needed to plunder, to possess, but she'd claimed control again already. Claimed him in a way he couldn't stop and didn't want to. Her muscles milked him—her silken heat invoking waves of pleasure. He should be dead already—heart attack. Instead, he was motivated to make it every damned bit as good for her.

After, as they breathed hard, the final moments of the race commentary rang in the room. She turned her head, her hair hiding her face from him, and looked at the screen as the podium celebration began. Massimo didn't release her and after a moment she relaxed.

'How did you end up being his guardian?' she asked as on the screen Emiliano was drenched in champagne. 'Doesn't he have family in Italy?'

He should welcome her curiosity as a win; instead, he felt edgy. He didn't discuss his family, but he had to answer her; honesty in this might help her trust him.

'His mother is in Italy, yes. Her husband was my mother's brother. There's wider family, too.' He drew a breath. 'Emiliano has precocious talent, you've seen it.'

'Yes.'

'There was so much extra pressure because he comes from a line of drivers. He showed his potential when he was very young and his father was unbelievably fast.'

'Was?' Her voice dropped. 'Don't tell me it was an accident.'

'No,' he assured her swiftly.

He knew she understood the immense, *endless* agony of an accident, but Massimo had the unbearable guilt of causing one, too.

'Cancer,' he clarified. 'Undetectable until it was too late. A lot of unscrupulous and pushy players circled around Emiliano, wanting to lock him into contracts. His mother and I agreed it was better to have him with me at Hearnshawe. I promised him that if he continued with his education, I'd build him the fastest car to ever hit the grid. I wanted him to be in a place where he could be protected, rather than pushed too soon.'

Lily sat back and looked him square in the eyes. 'He was on the grid the day he turned eighteen. How much sooner could he make it?'

'It's later than the rival teams would have had him,' he pointed out wryly. They'd wanted to get special dispensation. At the time he wanted to take it.'

'But you didn't let that happen?'

'Believe it or not, I'm too cautious.' He smiled. 'Emiliano wants to go fast in everything. 'There are still times when I have to step in. A lot of temptations are thrown at him.'

Guilt rippled. It had been because of Emiliano's vulnerability that he'd been on that cargo plane. But she never, ever needed to know that. It was irrelevant now.

'I don't want him taken advantage of,' he sighed. 'I would do anything to help him.'

He'd put in good support for Emiliano. Trainer. Psychologist. Nutritionist. The kid had thrived at his English estate and honestly, Massimo had figured he would take over the entire company eventually. Maybe he still would if this child didn't want to. Massimo intended to do the same for Lily and the baby. Housekeeper, nanny all the help she needed. He was very good at employing the absolute best.

'But you keep your distance from him during race weekends.' She tucked her hair behind her ears.

Had she noticed that? 'It's better for him to be focused,' he explained. 'Not feel additional pressure by having me breathing down his neck.'

She shook her head slightly and her eyes softened.

'You're stressed watching him. Every time. But it's so much safer than it used to be.'

'I don't need you to reassure me, Lily,' he muttered edgily. 'You do know I lobbied for the latest safety changes.'

'Yes.' She smiled gently. 'I do know that.'

He ran his tongue over his dry lips. 'Because you also know my parents died in a crash.'

Not on track, but in the *rain*.

She nodded. Silence expanded between them. He'd left so much unsaid, but he would never discuss that day.

He cleared his throat. 'We should shower before the doctor arrives.'

Lily ruffled her hair and shot Massimo a rueful grin. 'I only needed a doctor, not Singapore's best obstetrician and half his team to turn up. There weren't enough chairs in the room.'

Massimo offered her a glass of juice. He'd clearly been on a room service ordering spree again. She took it and settled onto one of the sun loungers, unable to resist the dish of nuts located conveniently near.

'I'm glad to know you're in excellent health,' he muttered softly.

'The results of the blood tests will take a few days.'

'We don't need to wait until then to make plans,' he said, then shot her a conciliatory smile. 'Though we can if you want.'

She rolled her eyes. Going slow wasn't in his repertoire.

In an ideal world, family ought to be close. Children treasured. This baby was a *gift* and she didn't want it to pick up on conflict between its parents. The timing might be terrible, their compromise difficult given their disparate wealth and power, but surely they *could* make this work without a wedding. Hell, maybe once they got this chemistry out of their systems they could even be friends.

Her heart puckered and she shrank into the seat. The fact was she *would* step back from his life and be safe in hers. Only now she couldn't help wondering what it could be like if he weren't so beyond her reach. And she couldn't resist indulging in a moment of curious fantasy. 'What would you do if you weren't Massimo Hearnshawe?'

'What's the point in wondering that? I *am* Massimo Hearnshawe.'

'Humour me.' What kind of life would he want?

'Why would you think I'd want a wildly different life to the one I have now?' He picked up a drink but didn't sip. 'Do you think I'm unhappy? I'm hardly working at gunpoint. I already have everything I've ever wanted.' He paused. 'Now, thanks to you, I'll have a wife and heir shortly, too.'

'But you didn't want those before.' He would have them already if that was the case. Had he ever wanted a family in the future?

He dropped his gaze. 'I imagined Emiliano would take over eventually.'

So that was a no. Why? Surely, a man in his position would want companionship—an heir. But there was hurt in him. Deep hurt.

'If you're so happy to be Massimo Hearnshawe, why didn't you tell me you were him when we flew back from Canada?'

'I didn't want anything to stop what was happening between us.'

She would have stopped had she known. *Maybe.* 'You're sure that I'd have recognised your name?'

'Darling, you were wearing my team cap,' he muttered.

The light amusement softened the defensive edge in him. She quickly sipped her juice to cover her melt. She'd been starved of affection for too long if a single *darling* could have this effect on her.

He sat down on the edge of her sun lounger and picked up her hand. 'If I could do anything, I would still work with the cars. I love their sleek beauty—low to the ground, slimline with subtle curves, screamingly fast, sensitive to the slightest touch, fiery and difficult to control. All responsive strength and power.' He slid his fingers up her arm as he spoke, teasing ever so lightly.

'That's what you find irresistible, huh?' She covered his hand with hers, trapping it right over her breast.

'Yes. There's nothing more beautiful.' He fluttered his fingers and shot her a wicked grin. 'What would you do if you weren't Lily Jones, Hearnshawe Racing mechanic?'

She shook her head. 'Working in P1 Global is my absolute dream. I would still strive to get there.'

'And Hearnshawe was your first pick.'

Even though he was right, she couldn't resist slapping his royal smugness down. 'Actually, I really wanted to get into Fournier, but my French isn't any good.'

He chuckled. 'So you were reduced to joining us.'

She'd never thought she'd actually be offered the job. 'Derek encouraged me to apply. My quitting will let him down.'

She felt bad at that prospect. Derek had been happy

for her to stay while she'd succeeded at the track, but now might be different. Now he and Jean mightn't want to see her anymore. She couldn't have a baby in the caravan anyway. She would need her own place. Independent from everyone—*especially* Massimo.

'You don't need to quit,' Massimo said, all teasing tone gone. 'Sure, you might need a break when you're too pregnant to fit beneath the car, but there's more than one job you could do at Hearnshawe.'

'I'm not interested in anything I haven't *earned*,' she muttered. That would be worse. Only tolerated in the factory because he'd knocked her up? That would be horrendous.

'No nepotism?' he said quietly. 'As little help as possible?'

She stared at him. He was still acting as if their wedding was a foregone conclusion. Driving the boat straight towards the iceberg with unbelievable, unrelenting arrogance and optimism, so certain he would get his way. But marriage was a step too far for her. She knew love had to be constantly earned and could easily be withheld—or worse, lost forever. Nothing was guaranteed. Just because she was having his baby didn't mean they had to be *together*. Just because they had chemistry now didn't mean it would last. Just because he was interested, patient, *amusing...*

She worried she wasn't capable of earning anyone's love, let alone *keeping* it. And worst of all, she didn't want to *have* to earn it. She just simply, baldly, wanted it no matter what. *Her* heart wasn't strong enough to cope with anything less than unconditional—and that was pure fairy tale.

'I need my independence,' she said.

'The thing is if you marry me you'll have more independence than you've ever known.'

She laughed abruptly, hiding the hurt welling up within her because she was finally beginning to see that he and she had completely different ideas about what marriage even meant.

'You're the bossiest person I've ever met,' she said. 'Which ought to be impossible given how domineering my dad is.'

'I won't be bossy once you agree,' he tempted. 'You'll have the freedom to do anything you want—you could have your own garage, Lily.'

'Freedom within a framework?' she mocked. 'No. Total independence is my default setting.'

'Settings can be adjusted,' he said. 'Why not change gear? Rebuild even?'

Because you couldn't rebuild something that had been completely broken.

CHAPTER NINE

Massimo glanced up as a shadow broke the light, impeding his vision. 'You shouldn't be awake.'

'I think that's my line,' she countered dryly. 'You realise it's three a.m.'

He gestured to the table. 'I had some work to do.'

'Yeah, the three-screen setup doesn't give it away at all. So much for taking a break, or am I the only one required to do that?'

Massimo silenced the incoming call and flipped his phone screen side down. Somehow, he would fit all the damned demands in, but the only ones he *wanted* to deal with this second were hers.

'Don't you need to answer it?' She moved closer.

Not when she was all fiery challenge. 'I'll phone them back later.'

'You should have more free time than anyone. You could have any number of managers in place.'

'I do, but there are a lot of companies to oversee and ultimately the buck stops with me.'

'Or maybe you like being so busy there isn't time for anything else.'

No, generally, there wasn't anything else he wanted to do. He didn't like to stop, definitely not be left with nothing but his thoughts. But Lily, as always, provoked him. 'I like being with you.'

That was the irony. That was why he was up working now. Her calling him on it made him confront the fact that he didn't want to miss a moment during the day with her. For the first time, work wasn't his entire life; it was interfering with it.

'You like having *sex* with me,' she corrected.

He smiled even as he felt outrage rise. Because whilst true, it was also unfair. She liked that every bit as much as he did.

She tightened her silk robe as she tilted her nose slightly in the air. 'I don't expect you to be by my side twenty-four-seven. That would be too much.'

Would it? He would have agreed with her only days ago, but disturbingly, the prospect didn't feel like *too much* now.

'You don't need to sacrifice sleep because you think I'll be unhappy if you don't spend every waking moment trying to make my life complete,' she added sassily. 'You don't need to *entertain* me.'

Oh so he was trying too hard? He didn't think so. He knew she *liked* him entertaining her. It was what she wanted now. But her insistence that she didn't need his attention all the hours of the day ought to please him. That she understood the world, the constraints and demands on his time, meant their marriage might actually work. The company would always come first for him. It had to. But instead of appreciating her acceptance of the limitations on his time, he was unaccountably irked. He stood and slowly advanced towards her, watching the signs of her ignition. 'So you don't want me to entertain you now?'

Her breathing quickened. 'Not when you have more important things to do. I wouldn't want to be too demanding. Your previous partners must have been very high maintenance.'

Well, he'd never bothered to sit up late to get work done just to have more time for a woman before.

'Partners?' he teased her.

'Girlfriends, lovers…' She looked awkward.

'You think there have been a few?'

She pressed her lips together. 'Have you really not slept with anyone in ages?'

'Why wouldn't you believe me? You're the same.'

'But I'm not…' She huffed out a sigh. 'You have a lot going for you.'

'You mean money.'

'Amongst other things,' she mumbled endearingly.

'No lovers. Not even any princesses. I promise.' He'd been jealous of every guy who got to work with her in the garage. Even his own cousin. 'I dated in the past but it's amazing how many people don't like how much time it takes to oversee a conglomerate.'

Her eyes narrowed. 'You're saying they got bored and didn't stick around?'

'Even the ones determined to give me a long leash eventually get fed up with the other demands on my time.' He reached for her hand.

'Leash?' Her eyebrows shot up. 'Oh then please, let me give you a leash long enough to reach the moon.'

'*This* is why you'll make the perfect wife.' He laughed and tugged her to the sofa and sat her on his lap. 'Were *your* previous lovers demanding?'

'My one boyfriend was my older brother's friend, so you know who he chose.'

His anger rippled. One boyfriend. *Years* ago. She'd been alone so long.

'Why has there been no one else since him?' He kissed across her collarbones. 'Why no other little snack?'

She shrugged. 'I was busy.'

Building her career, her security. But no wonder she'd been so keen that night on the plane and he'd never felt so lucky that she'd deigned to choose him. Why couldn't she see that he could give her career and security *and* damned hot sex? 'Lily—'

'Shhh.' She brushed her lips against his. 'Don't talk. I just want to—'

Massimo braced, breathless as she did what she wanted.

'Are you using sex to avoid further conversation?' he teased.

She shot him a look—a contrary mix of hedonism and hidden hurt. 'As if you're devastated.'

Lily lifted her arms to the sky, leaning from one side to the other, stretching the kinks from her spine.

'What are you doing?'

She turned and saw Massimo settling into a sun lounger up on the deck. She'd thought he might sleep in.

'Callisthenics, some weights, then a twenty-minute swim,' she answered.

The pool had a resistance setting so she could swim for ages and get nowhere, and she'd gotten a yoga mat and some weights delivered to the villa and set up a small circuit.

'In a bikini?'

'Why not?' She eyed him defensively; she didn't want him suggesting she shouldn't overexert herself in the heat. 'I'm building my muscles. I need to prove my strength if I'm to make it into the pit crew.'

He opened his mouth. Closed it. Clearly thinking before speaking. 'You've been told you're not strong enough?'

'So many times it's very boring.'

'Yet, motivating because you can't resist defying convention.' He frowned. 'None of our female mechanics have made it into pit crew. Do you think it's gender bias?'

'Maybe.' She swung her arms in opposite circles. 'It's ironic when you consider that women *are* stronger than men.' She caught his raised brows. 'Generally, we live longer. Case closed.'

'But Lily…' He looked mournful. 'Would you really want to live without me?'

'I can't wait to.'

'Yet, you want to stand in front of a car hurtling towards you at eighty kilometres an hour?'

'You know how good the brakes are.' She sighed and swung her arms the other way. 'Obviously not while I'm pregnant. But just because I'm pregnant doesn't mean I can't maintain my strength.' She paused as he slipped his T-shirt off and settled back bare chested in the sun. 'Are you sure you don't want to move inside? I wouldn't want to get your laptop wet.'

'You won't,' he said softly. 'I can safely read my report from here.'

His sunglasses didn't hide the fact that he was watching her. Avidly.

Lily lifted her head and flaunted her flexibility as well as her strength—yes, she showed off, feeling a provocative sensuality as she moved. But he didn't move; he was rock still while she grew increasingly hot. In the end she had to dive into the cool water far sooner than planned. Even then she was aware of him *still* watching as she swam. In minutes she gave up and rested her arms on the side of the pool and watched him watching her.

'How far through your report did you get?' She smirked.

'How far through your twenty minutes did you get?' he countered, but then slammed the lid of his laptop shut. 'It's impossible to get anything done when you're around to watch.'

A bubble of joy rose within her. His haste mirrored her need exactly. She wanted him—now, always. He hauled her out of the pool, as decisive, intense, driven as ever. Her limbs liquefied as he kissed her. Her knees weakened, her body becoming a pliable mass in the languid heat. She loved learning how to do the same to him— seeking out his vulnerable points, discovering the preferences he couldn't hide—the sudden clench of jaw, the agonised groan he could no longer contain. These were all *wins* for her. He was as alone as she, but just for now they could have this; she would make the most of every moment she could. She caressed him, indulging every decadent sense until stark need gripped them both until they were lost in that mindless storm of ecstasy. Then she pressed her face to his chest, hiding how increasingly vulnerable she felt in the aftermath. She didn't ask how long they were staying in their gorgeous little villa. She didn't *want* to know and she was very happy to use sex to avoid serious discussion.

Except it wasn't avoidance; it was rapidly becoming addiction and it was absolutely becoming a problem.

Massimo reworked his routine. He remained in bed until she woke, then made the most of her snuggly hot morning mood. After breakfast, she worked out by the pool. He'd been aware of her athleticism—he'd repeatedly explored her slim, supple, strong body—but watching her physical training was a delicious torment now he indulged in daily. She did it as she did everything else—with full-bore intensity.

He burned through as much work as was humanly possible in as short of a time he could. It was a far reduced schedule, but still too onerous and he was increasingly annoyed by the requests for him to get back to the office. Any one of the offices—even the one in Singapore. A bunch of invitations clogged his inbox. He didn't answer any. Instead, he couldn't resist joining her on the sofa, and the afternoons vanished in replays of races and technical analyses. They debated best track, greatest ever driver, overtake of the season thus far. Her knowledge didn't just rival his, but possibly surpassed it. Though as neither of them were inclined to concede an inch, it made for passionate arguments only to be resolved via physical domination.

Three days had passed like this and now he pounced the second she appeared from her post-swim shower. 'Help me choose the colour scheme for the interior of the new coupe.'

She looked startled. 'Are you serious?'

'Come and see.' He gestured to his computer. 'My current dilemma is choosing between this periwinkle or this sky blue.'

'Peri-what?' She laughed. 'So you act as if you're exceptionally busy making company decisions so big they take up three screens, but you're actually just studying colour swatches?'

'They're vital. Form and beauty matter.' He genuinely wanted her opinion, but apparently, she was still stuck on the fact that this was an actual question. 'And my spreadsheets *are* very big, hence the three screens. I always get the final say on colours for all of the products.'

'*This* is what keeps you up at three a.m.? Massimo, this is mastery-level micromanagement.'

'There have to be some perks,' he said. Never would he admit what demons really kept him awake. He'd never regretted the mistakes of his past as much as he did now.

'Perks. You're really serious? They're almost identical.' She looked from the screen to him and back again and sighed. 'The cornflower.' She pointed to the right. 'The other one—'

'Periwinkle—'

'Is a bit purple.'

'Hmm.' He cocked his head and considered them both again for a long moment. 'What?' He turned as she giggled.

'You're really invested in decisions this microscopic.'

As she smiled, his damned chest tightened. Her vibrancy hummed, enveloping him in satisfaction. He'd achieved his goal—she'd recovered from that extreme tiredness. Sleeping longer, eating well, exercising; these

few days had been hugely beneficial. They could probably go home soon.

'We should go out this afternoon,' he suggested im-
pulsively.

'What?' She stiffened. 'Why? I don't have anything
to wear.'

'Such resistance,' he teased. Naturally, her quick shut-
down and weak excuse had him challenging her. 'When
were you last in Singapore? Let's go explore.'

'Are you sure you can drag yourself away from the
periwinkle decision?'

Hearnshawe was everything, but for just a little longer, it could wait.

He took her to the Gardens by the Bay. She marvelled
at the scope of it—the majestic plantings and the geo-
metric glasshouses. The famous Supertrees were a stunning mix of technology and nature and simply dwarfed
her. She darted through the lush space, her bright smile
fitting perfectly in the fascinating environment. When it
got too warm to walk the skyway he drew her into the
enormous flowerdome. A vast collection of delicate orchids was the initial display.

'They're such beautiful colours,' he murmured as they
walked amongst them.

'Do they inspire you for the car interiors?' she teased.

'Many things inspire me.'

Lily suddenly sped forward. 'Oh look at the butterfly.'

Amused by her high-speed excitement, he laced his
fingers through hers; getting her to slow down wasn't
easy. 'It might come to you, if you stay still.'

She obediently paused. The butterfly danced between
them—fragile, vibrant, vulnerable, too quick to catch.

Just like her. The delicate creature grazed the back of her hand and hovered near for a few moments.

At a high-pitched gurgle of delight, they both turned. A family was behind them—parents with their three small children who ran, fast and excited. Lily's smile turned tender as they passed her. Massimo stilled as he was struck by a vision of the future—Lily chasing after an elfin-featured toddler—smiling like that at the lucky little thing.

'We'll bring our baby back here,' he muttered.

Her head whipped up and the butterfly hovering about her took flight in a fast flutter of colour. 'Is that how you see us? A happy family, all smiles and sunshine?'

He froze. It had been an image, an instant, gone in a puff. He'd not considered his words before they'd slipped out, but now he did. The truth was he couldn't follow through. She ought to know that and why.

'Is that what your parents had?' she added.

He owed her an honest answer. Biting the inside of his lip, he focused on the deep green foliage, avoiding the softness he knew would be in her eyes.

'They didn't marry until I was nearly nine,' he answered lightly. 'I spent the first eight years of my life with my mother in Italy. The Costa family are full motorhead, generations of mechanics and drivers. They live five minutes from one of the most famous circuits in the world. Dad went there on a research trip, met my mother, had an affair...' He shrugged. 'Unfortunately, he was engaged to another woman at the time so I spent years with other kids whispering about the rich guy who came to visit my mother and me but who didn't ever stay, didn't ever claim us as *his*.' He'd felt such shame. 'I'd like to avoid adding that unnecessary complication to our child's life.'

'But our child can have your name. It shouldn't matter what people think.'

'Says the woman whose main argument is that her family isn't respectable enough for me to marry into.' He turned to face her.

'That's different. My lot could make things actually *difficult*.'

No, they wouldn't. Massimo was already on to that. But *that* was definitely a conversation for another day. He needed to get her on board with their future first.

'*We* can handle difficult,' he said. 'Our *child* shouldn't have to.'

'But there'll be *pressure*. To be the heir to the Hearnshawe empire? Would you want our baby to be a driver, or the next CEO? You've got awfully big shoes to fill, Massimo.'

'That Hearnshawe pressure can't be avoided whether or not we're married. In fact, it's why it's even more important that we *are*.' He was certain of it. 'I want our child to be free to find their own purpose. It'll be up to them to choose whether that's within Hearnshawe Group, but they'll need to be able to handle their heritage. When you have immense privilege, you *have* to learn how to deal with it.'

'Or?'

'It'll mess you up.' He was messed up. He *had* messed up.

She was quiet. Waiting. He met her unspoken query with a sigh.

'It took Dad far too long to stand up to my grandfather and call off the other engagement,' he said.

'Your *grandfather*?' Lily's jaw dropped.

'He had an iron grip on everything, bit like your father. There was only one way things should be done and it was his. He wanted Dad to marry someone else. Dad caved and got engaged but stalled on the wedding for years. In the end, marrying my mother and bringing us to Hearnshawe was the only fight he ever won against the old guy.'

'How did it finally happen after so long?'

Massimo stared at the delicate orchids, but barely saw them. 'You have to understand. Dad was such a dreamer. He had all kinds of innovative ideas, especially regarding safety standards, but my grandfather saw safety as weak, somehow watering down the spice in racing. He wouldn't give his ideas a chance. He belittled him over every last little thing and rubbished him for not being forceful enough. When Hearnshawe began to decline, that only made him dig his heels in more. He wouldn't listen to anyone, not even experts.' He'd been a domineering, blinkered bully. 'When Dad saw me karting in Italy as a kid, he realised I could be a driver. If I won championships in his cars for Hearnshawe, he would finally get the old man's attention and maybe he'd consider the broader changes my father wanted to make within the company.'

'So your dad only brought you to Hearnshawe once you'd shown you could drive?' Lily's voice was thin.

Massimo stiffened. 'It wasn't that callous. He and I... It was our thing.' He paused. 'Outwardly, my grandfather welcomed us, but privately he still didn't accept it. He constantly questioned if I was *truly* a Hearnshawe. Apparently, I didn't act like one. I was too impulsive and wilful. Even my success in racing raised his doubts—how could my *father* have a son who drove so fast? In the privacy of the estate, he fully questioned paternity. He was awful to my father and awful about him. He told me that Dad had been unfaithful to Mum through the years, that I wasn't the *only* bastard, just the eldest and the only one with any driving talent. He was constantly cruel.' He bent his head. 'He undermined Dad so much. I understand *how* Dad was weakened in the way he was.'

'What about you?' she asked. 'Were you weakened?'

'I was thrust into a world where I could suddenly have everything I wanted. At the time, that was to race. I was officially a Hearnshawe. I was fast and I was *special* and I wasn't letting that old jerk or anyone else stop me.' He bitterly mocked the idiocy and arrogance of his youth. 'I thought I was better than anyone, that I could do anything I wanted, and I did.' He looked at her. 'You were right about me. I was shockingly spoiled then.'

There was a sharp silence. He turned towards her.

Lily's gaze skittered away from his and he saw her swallow. 'What about your mother? Was she happy to have married him at last? To move to England?'

'I don't know if it was true about other women, but from what I saw they *were* happy,' he said huskily. Every visit in the early years, there had been laughter. 'I think if he'd had the courage, Dad would have moved to Italy, but he couldn't find it. And as I got older, she wanted better opportunities for me.'

'Ones that could be found with Hearnshawe.'

He nodded. 'She encouraged Dad to work on those safety designs. She believed in him. Her father was a test driver who crashed when she was in her teens. She knew about other accidents. She was particularly paranoid about racing in the rain.' He drew in a difficult breath. 'Her father had died in the rain.'

'Oh no.' Lily wrapped her arms around herself. 'No wonder you were stressed during the storm in qualifying the other day.'

'And when you were on the track. I know you think I overreacted, but it hit old wounds.'

'Your parents' accident.'

'Mine, too.' Massimo lifted his hand to show her the scars on either side of his forearm. 'Shattered both ulna and radius. The bone broke through the skin.'

'It must've been painful.'

The physical pain hadn't been enough. He'd deserved so much more.

'It was a private practice karting session. I was spoiled enough to have them all the time. Mum phoned and flipped out about the weather but I was arrogant enough to think I could master it and angry at her interference. We argued, I hung up on her, determined to prove her wrong. But on track I lost focus, spun out and flipped. I was thrown from the kart and landed badly. Crushed a couple of ribs as well as the arm. But they weren't life-altering injuries. Aside from the scar, I've no permanent damage. I recovered full physical strength after a couple of months.'

'And raced again?'

'No,' he whispered. 'I didn't know that Mum was so upset she'd decided to come to the track to stop me. Dad got in the car, too. It wasn't a long trip but a driver coming the other way skidded onto their side of the road. There was nothing they could have done.'

'Their accident was *that* same day?' Lily paled.

Their accident was his fault entirely. He stepped forward, taking hold of the barrier blocking off the viewing area. 'I was in the hospital waiting for surgery, waiting for my parents to come and say *I told you so*. Instead, my grandfather arrived and informed me that my parents' bodies had just been brought into the morgue. Then he told me I would *never* be a driver for Hearnshawe. I would never fulfil my father's ambition. I would never be a *winner*. As if I cared at that point.' He gripped the rail more tightly. 'But he was right. I would never race again.'

'You made a vow,' she murmured.

Right.

She gently covered his hand with hers. 'You were only a child, Massimo.'

'I was thirteen.' Old enough and it was no excuse. He didn't relax. He couldn't. 'My grandfather was right about several things. I *was* hot-headed. I was wilful and impetuous. I shouldn't have been out there that day and certainly not after Mum told me not to. But I was defiant and angry. There's no room for emotion on track. *Everyone* makes mistakes when emotions are engaged.'

He was better off without them. He'd made mistake after mistake until he'd learned that keeping cool, calm, *remote* was everything. Emotions had to be controlled. Dealt with later—or ideally never at all. Just thinking about this had his stomach churning and cold sweat of regret slicking his skin.

'You were left with *him*. Your grandfather.'

'As I was all that was left, he became determined to make me into the man he'd failed to make my father into. I let him. I got disciplined, got grades, learned everything

I could from him about the business. Because I'd decided I would do all the things my father had wanted to do at Hearnshawe. I would enact the reforms *he'd* dreamed of. I decided to take everything from my grandfather and I did. I took revenge for the way he'd treated my father for all those years.'

'So it's true you locked him out of the premises?'

'It was billed as a ruthless takeover of the entire operation that destroyed the man, but while I did lock him out, it was only from the factory. He still had his home and several millions. It was time for him to enjoy those, retire and live well rather than slowly grinding Hearnshawe into dust.'

'Did he ever forgive you for it?'

'When he saw the sales figures, I got a call inviting me to dinner. I didn't go.'

'Did you ever forgive him?'

'No. And while I'll never race for Hearnshawe, a Costa now does, which is an unintended bonus that made the old bastard deeply unhappy.' He stiffened, taking his hand from under hers and turning to make sure she understood. 'That's not why I brought Emiliano to England. If he wanted to stop racing tomorrow, that'd be fine. I won't let *anyone* take advantage of him, including myself.'

'I know that. I know you care about him.'

Right. He'd helped Emiliano. He would help her child, too. He could set him up in the same way.

'Do you think it was really revenge on your grandfather, or are you trying to make reparations to your parents?'

He slowly blinked, confused.

'You've done all the things your father had wanted to

do in the company,' she elaborated. 'You look after Emiliano for your mother. You want to make them both proud.'

'But I *can't*,' he argued hoarsely. They were dead because of him. 'I destroyed so much.' There was more that he could never, ever make right.

'Mum was *pregnant*.' The words slipped from him in a breathless slide of agony. 'They'd not told anyone, but that morning they told me I'd be getting a baby brother. Mum was so happy but I was so self-involved, all I wanted was to get to the track so I could practice, and I didn't give a damn about that or bother checking the weather forecast.'

'Massimo.' She moved closer and gripped his hands. 'You can't blame yourself.'

Of course he could. What he *couldn't* do was change what had happened.

Her eyes were huge and soft. He bent his head to avoid them, appalled as emotion overwhelmed him. He clamped every muscle in his body, stopping the shaking. Stopping the *feeling*.

'I'm so sorry you lost your parents,' she said. 'I'm sorry you never got your brother.'

She leaned against him and he stiffened even more. But she just rested against him—not with all of her weight, but all of her warmth. She simply stayed close so that in this moment, as memory burned, he was not alone. All he could do was breathe. Slowly, the intense horror sank back down—a bedrock of remorse buried so deep in his gut that he could never get rid of it. He had no right to even want to—the recklessness of that day was something he would live with forever.

Lily had lost a brother, too. She'd lost her whole life

when her family had rejected her. So she knew there was nothing to say to make it better.

But the difference was his brother's death was his fault. The child hadn't even had the chance to live. He couldn't make those kinds of mistakes again.

He clenched his muscles and stepped back from her. 'We should get back to the hotel.'

She nodded and said nothing. He was a jerk. This was supposed to have been a relaxing sightseeing trip. A chance to see a little of Singapore before they had to go home, and he'd just dumped his emotional baggage all over her.

'I'll order dinner,' he said the second they got back to the villa.

He walked to the hotel reception completely unnecessarily, to make the order and wait for it. When he got back she was at the table, writing in her fat notebook.

He set the containers on the table. 'Is it a diary?'

'You think I'm pouring my feelings onto paper?' Her smile was teasing but wariness lingered in her eyes.

He shook his head slowly. No, she kept them to herself. The only time he had any idea where he stood with her was when they were in bed. She flipped the notebook so he could see the pages. The graph paper was filled with sketches, equations, notes, reminders.

'You make notes on the cars?'

'You were right,' she said. 'I can't work in a garage when I'm enormous. I'll tip over. So I'm going to design racing cars and by that I don't mean choose the livery colour scheme.' She shot him a teasing smile. 'I want to study engineering. I have to do a bridging course first, so it's going to take a while, but I'm going to do it.'

'I believe you.' He had no doubt that one day people would pay millions to get their hands on her notebook. But she was talking about *years* of study. Especially if she did it part-time. The realisation pleased him immeasurably.

'You can do all your internships at Hearnshawe,' he said huskily. 'Whichever division you want. We have all the toys. I can help.'

'I know. Thank you.'

He gaped. This was a major breakthrough. The first glimmer of acceptance that their futures were entwined. Had it come only about because he'd told her about his parents? Had he manipulated her—albeit unintentionally? He never should have burdened her with the detail of his mother's pregnancy. No one had ever needed to know the depths of that pain. He'd not done it to try to convince her to accept him. Honestly, he still didn't know how it had spilled out. Suddenly hot, his skin prickled.

'Don't concede anything because you feel sorry for me. Because of what I said. I just don't want this child to go through any...'

He'd wanted her to understand why he'd been freaked out by her driving in the rain. Why he felt the bone-deep need to protect her and the baby. Why he needed to damned well do *better*.

She moved nearer. 'It's helped me understand why you feel such responsibility for everything. I'm glad you trusted me enough to tell me. But it doesn't change my view on what we should do in our future.' Her gaze melted. 'You don't need to feel more guilt, Massimo. We'll just have to work harder to reach a compromise.'

'How are we going to do that when you're more stubborn than a mule?'

Her radiant smile appeared. 'And you're more determined than a donkey?'

He couldn't smile back. The brief balm her quietly empathetic support had given him before was washed away by a wave of bitterness and self-recrimination. He'd not been entirely honest with her. The fact that he'd not confessed why he'd been on that cargo plane nagged. He ignored it. That secret he had to keep. He couldn't risk losing her trust *now*. She still believed she wasn't suitable and knowing he'd once been suspicious would hardly help. Maybe he would show her how well she could fit within his world.

'I've been invited to a party in the city tomorrow night,' he muttered. 'That white number you wore at the team party would be perfect.'

'Would it?' She shot him an arch look. 'So you're dictating both my attendance and my dress?'

Yeah, he'd known she'd bite at that. But she'd already said she had little to wear and he wasn't making the mistake of offering to buy her an outfit. Surely, she wasn't insecure in herself in being seen with him. 'Honestly, anything would be perfect but as you're determined to pretend you can't handle social occasions, I was trying to reassure you.'

'I don't need reassurance.'

'Great, so you'll come with me.'

'You're deliberately provoking me.'

'Is it working?'

She studied her notebook. 'Will there be dancing?'

'I'll dance with you whether there's music or not.' The

selfish, impetuous, hothead within just wanted a little more time with her.

'Okay, then.'

He should have been pleased. He should have felt satisfaction that she was beginning to accept his offerings, that maybe soon she'd say *yes*. Instead, he only felt increasing stress. He pulled her closer, silencing his brain by activating his body.

'Am I getting a bonus because I said yes to you?' She called him on it.

'No. *I'm* getting a bonus because I haven't the strength to resist.'

CHAPTER TEN

LILY SWAM AGAINST the resistance, but burning her energy with a tough swim to nowhere wasn't enough to stop her overthinking. She hadn't lied. She wouldn't concede anything, wouldn't change the course of her life and agree to matrimony just because he'd told her something terrible. But that he'd told her something at *all* softened her defences against him. Every moment she spent with him led her more and more into *like*. She didn't just relish their moments in bed, she adored every other second as well. Sure, he was outrageously bossy and she knew he had a ruthless streak, but knowing more about *why* he'd become like that helped. He wasn't the cold, unfeeling CEO she'd once thought. Grief and guilt were terrible twin burdens. Trite words couldn't heal wounds like his. Nor would an ill-considered marriage. She wished he'd understand that he didn't need to feel responsible for *her*.

But he did. That was why he was being gentle with her. Spoiling her with time, his attention, delectable food and drink and sensual delights. He wasn't seducing her, he was lulling her. Normalising indulgence and making her feel safe and lazy enough not to argue anymore. To agree. It was a carefully considered strategy. But it *was* a strategy and he was only doing it because she was pregnant.

She had to work harder to resist *him*.

She'd stayed with him in Singapore because she'd wanted to resolve their situation. Her baby deserved to have both parents in its life and she'd wanted to work this out amicably. But he was so very challenging, so very charming. He made her laugh, made her feel seen and heard and *alive*. The idea of happy family times—trips to playgrounds, parks—was so tempting. She'd not had a childhood filled with those things and like Massimo, she wanted the best for this baby. She even understood that their child would need guidance in handling the Hearnshawe pressures and privileges. But he'd had enough turmoil in his private life and she wasn't adding to it with her equally messed-up family. She wouldn't cause him more trouble.

She and Massimo could manage everything necessary with a co-parenting situation. Everything could be in a *contract*. But that was the difference between her and him. Massimo saw their marriage *itself* as a contract, nothing more. Whereas marriage for Lily meant something else. Something idealistic and romantic and impossible. All sorts of emotions swirled within her. She had the horrible feeling she felt more for him than like. She was horribly afraid she was falling in—

No. She couldn't believe that. She couldn't *trust* her own emotions. And she certainly couldn't emotionally invest in someone who didn't *want* to love her back. She already had an entire family who didn't love her back. Massimo had never actually wanted to marry anyone and she couldn't marry him without risking her vulnerable heart too much.

Because she already liked him far too much. *More* than liked him.

She rolled to her back and glanced up to the deck. He was on a lounger there, frowning at his tablet. They couldn't stay in Singapore much longer. He was working slightly longer each day and his phone was ringing more frequently—with him looking more harried with each interruption. He worked too hard. She rolled back and kept swimming.

She'd worked almost all her life. In her parents' garage, then on her own. She'd kept her distance from her colleagues, knowing if she ever were to mix work with pleasure that she would lose her job. Indeed, that was what had happened now. But she would rebuild her future and yes, she would let him help. She honestly had little choice about that. But eventually, she would repay every penny of the fees and costs he would cover for her. She would have to for her own peace.

The party was in a few hours. Apparently, it was at a rooftop bar in the heart of Singapore. There would be drinks, canapes, *dancing*. Aside from him, no one who knew her would be there. Her family was on the other side of the world, and the P1 circus had long since left town. They would be out but almost unseen.

She looked at Massimo again. He'd fallen asleep on the lounger. She smiled, happy to see him fully relaxed. It didn't happen all that often.

She got out of the pool and wrapped in a large towel. She'd bought a dress online and had it delivered to their hotel—spending a little of her savings just for the sassy joy of surprising him. She'd even made an appointment at the hotel beautician. Because tonight was going to be *hers*.

She would be his partner out in public just this once—it was private enough for her to risk. Then, for her own protection, their sexual intimacy had to end. They would go back to England; she would stay strong. They would parent as allies—she would survive it. That was what she did.

But before she had to face all that difficulty, she couldn't resist one last night of indulgence.

Massimo woke to silence. No gentle splash as Lily swam. His eyes shot open and he sat up. The water in the pool was still, while the area around it was completely dry. She'd not recently left it. Was it not the middle of the afternoon?

'Lily?' He went into the villa, suddenly chilled.

There wasn't some old race playing on the screen. Her notebook and pen were on the table, but she wasn't on the sofa. He stepped into the bedroom, but she wasn't resting in there, either. He glanced at his watch and realised it was far later than he'd thought. He went back to the deck for his phone. No message. No note.

Where was she? Had she left? No. Her bag was still here, her notebook. Even so, he panicked.

The door opened and he shot over. She walked in looking like sunshine. Her hair hung over her shoulders and her skin was burnished gold. He just gaped.

Her eyebrows arched. 'What's wrong?'

Relief buffeted him so hard he had to lean a hand against the wall. *Damn.*

'Has something happened?' She frowned.

He cleared his throat and pulled out a smile. 'No, I just woke up.'

'You're breathing funny. Did you have a nightmare?'

Something like that.

'I went to the hotel spa. I didn't want to wake you.' She paused. 'Did you think I'd left? I wouldn't do that, Massimo. Don't you trust me at all yet?'

Did that mean she was starting to trust him?

'I just...'

Panicked upon waking.

Because yes, he'd thought she was gone. But it was his over-the-top reaction to her possible absence appalling him now. He shouldn't be this freaked out. 'Sometimes bad things happen.'

'Not today.' She smiled tightly. 'Do you still want to go out?'

He stared at her. She truly looked golden. He realised her makeup was done—her mouth was extra glossy. His lungs squeezed. Because she'd gone to the spa. She was always alluring, but she'd made an effort and he wasn't wasting it with some tragic overtired overreaction.

'Yes,' he growled huskily. He needed to get out of here. 'I'll just... I won't be long.'

'Okay. I'll get into my dress.'

He flicked the shower on freezing. He'd never before felt horror at being *alone*. He *liked* being alone. It was how he'd engineered his life. To focus on work. To be there when he had to be for Emiliano—but at a distance. But waking up and believing for a mere moment that Lily was gone? That had almost caused a heart attack. Her presence had become important to him.

No. The heat was getting to him or he was coming down with something. He was fine. He yanked on a suit, determined to get a grip. He was doing well. He'd juggled work and gotten an even more important deal over the line. She was thriving—hell, even in the few days they'd had here, her belly had rounded slightly. He had to get her to say yes to him so he could back the hell away.

She didn't believe that she was an appropriate fit for his life; taking her out he would show she was wrong. Brooding, he stalked out to the lounge, caught sight of her and almost fell over his feet.

'I'm a walking red flag,' she joked.

'It's not a stop signal you're sending me.'

'No?'

She wasn't wearing the white dress he'd expected. It was a red wisp designed to incite uncontrollable desire. It worked.

'Come on.' He had to get them out of there.

She was making a statement, just not the one she thought she was. She thought she wasn't an appropriate partner for him? That she was a danger? She couldn't look more perfect to him. He'd never been more grateful for an enormous car with a driver and a privacy screen he immediately enabled. Then he sat back and drank in the vitality in her eyes, her shining hair. God, she was blossoming.

'Your skin is gleaming,' he muttered.

'It's the beauty treatment.'

'Not the treatment.'

She tilted her head, studying him as much as he was studying her. Only she seemed a little more calm about it.

'Do you miss racing cars?' she suddenly asked.

He blinked. 'I don't have time to miss racing cars.'

An immediate deflection but she saw right through it.

'I think you do,' she whispered. 'You like to go fast.'

He lifted his collar away from his neck. Despite that

icy shower, he felt unbearably hot. He'd had moments of unrest in his life, but this was something else.

'You don't do many of the things you like,' she added. 'It's all for the company, never just for yourself.'

Oh she was *wrong*.

He leaned over and kissed her. Partly to silence her. Partly because he could no longer stop himself from doing the one thing he liked more than anything. But he fisted his hands, battling the impulse to fully stake his claim, to clamp her to his side so she couldn't ever escape. She was so tempting, more powerful than the most addictive drug. Damn it, he needed to regain his self-control. But she kissed him back. She didn't just kiss—she gave and he couldn't help but take.

'You wore this to deliberately torment me.' He succumbed and fingered the siren-red silk strap.

His anger, his need, rose. He would torment her as she tormented him. If they weren't driving, if there was no need for damned safety belts, he would have her astride him, riding him to oblivion in a heartbeat. Instead, he swooped over her, stroking, sliding his hands beneath her dress and over her hot body. The damned safety belt was suddenly useful for it kept her in place—hot and open to him. He teased her nipples to tight little peaks.

'This is madness,' she panted.

Ah, but she was close and that pushed him on. Lust-hazed need swept over him. He savoured her scent, sliding his tongue over her silky-smooth skin and nibbling at her sensitive tips. It was only *this*—only explosive, undeniable desire. But her little sob broke him wide-open and suddenly, all he wanted was to *see* her. He pressed his forehead against hers. Locked his eyes on hers. While her thighs locked on the hand he'd slid between them. But he could flick his fingers and he knew just how she liked him to. He needed to see pleasure smash over her in that unstoppable wave.

'Let it happen, sweetheart. Let me see you.'

He ached for her to take what little he could give her.

Her hands threaded through his hair, holding him close.

'You *always* see me,' she whispered. 'Always please me.'

Her words reverberated so deeply within him that he had to kiss her to stop their impact. But then her kiss sliced to his soul. And as he stroked, euphoria shuddered through her. He watched, ripped apart as she came hard, treasuring the vulnerability she displayed with him. This wasn't just sex; this was…*impossible.*

He couldn't let this matter this much. And he couldn't hold her like this forever.

Silently, he held her as the violence of her orgasm eased. Then she pushed back, tugging the silk back down.

'I can't believe I have to face people.' The flush in her cheeks deepened.

'You look stunning.'

There were more cameras than he expected. Members of the public with their phones up, video on. She bit her lip and stepped behind him. He wrapped his arm around her and drew her closer to mutter almost angrily in her ear. 'I'm not ashamed of you, Lily. I don't care who your parents are or what they have or haven't done.'

And he'd bought their silence to ensure her security. He would tell her that when they were alone again. She probably wouldn't be pleased. But she *never* ought to want to hide. She deserved so much *more* than that.

He was the one stained in everlasting shame. He grabbed her hand tightly, hiding his own shaking fingers.

Lily wasn't sure quite how she got up to the venue. Her legs had stopped trembling, but her heart was racing faster than a roadster on a hot lap. What had just happened? Why had that just happened? What was he *thinking*?

Bad things happen.

Had he actually meant that her *leaving* would be bad? Had he been that bothered? Because it seemed like he had. It seemed as if he'd suddenly dropped his facade and shown he cared. Did he, though? Could she believe that?

'Please, meet my partner, Lily.' Massimo smoothly introduced her to someone.

'Partner?' Lily echoed as they moved deeper into the room, trying to make light of it when in reality the prospect struck too deep. 'Is that you soft launching us?'

'That dress is no soft launch and you know it.'

What she'd thought she'd known was that there could be no *us*. Except within the past hour something seemed to have changed within Massimo. There was something wild and reckless about him and she couldn't quite keep up.

'Are you ready to dance with me?' He ran his fingers lightly down the side of her face.

Maybe it was only a thoughtless movement from him, but it felt like so much more for her. He pulled her straight onto the dance floor and into his arms. Because of course she followed. And of course he could dance—how was that possible when all he did was work? But he was lithe and graceful and quick. She was instantly lost in the heat, the fast beat, the glittering intensity in his eyes and that flash of a too-rare wide smile. She didn't want the moment to end. Dancing high enough to almost touch the sky, it was what dreams were made of.

But it was hot. Too hot.

'You need a drink?' he asked.

'Please.' She nodded, breathless. 'I'll wait here.'

By a fan funnelling blessedly cool air in her direction. She gazed across the skyline, taking in the light show flickering across several buildings and the vast expanse of water stretching for miles beyond. Then she turned and took in the polished and stunning dresses so many of the women were wearing. Distracted, she wondered why Massimo had reacted as weirdly as he had when he'd thought she'd left. Why he'd suddenly seemed to cut loose now. Very hot and dangerously happy, she was just getting her heart rate back to normal when Emiliano materialised in front of her.

'Ciao, Lily!' He beamed at her.

'Hi.' She gaped, then stammered thoughtlessly. 'I didn't know you'd be here tonight.'

He nodded affably. 'I holidayed in Japan, then came back for this before heading home.'

She pressed her hand to her chest, trying to stop her heart from thumping right out of it. She'd not expected anyone from Hearnshawe to be present tonight. Massimo can't have known, either, or he would have warned her, right? Or perhaps he *had* known and hadn't said anything because then she wouldn't have agreed to come. She glanced across the bar. She didn't see any other Hearnshawe people about, and an imperious-looking trio of businessmen had Massimo cornered.

'Congratulations on your podium.' She made herself focus on Emiliano. Honestly, she was curious about him. He'd spent his entire teen years under Massimo's roof and she wondered how close they were. 'May it be the first of many in P1.'

'Yes, indeed.' He nodded, all confidence. 'You arrived with Massimo, sì?' His smile broadened. 'Now I know why I'm not allowed to talk to you in the garage.'

'What? You're not what?'

'You never saw that video of us talking in the garage? It went viral.'

Did he mean them talking tyres in Singapore? Had someone filmed that?

'I'm not on social media,' she muttered.

No one had said anything to her about any viral video clip. Massimo certainly hadn't. It must've happened so quickly.

'Very wise.' Emiliano nodded. 'It set off the alarms because I got involved with an older woman a couple of years ago.'

'Oh?' Lily almost choked.

A couple of years ago Emiliano would have barely been seventeen. And why alarms that he'd talked to her? Surely, no one would have considered Lily to be a threat?

'It's embarrassing,' he said chattily. 'I fell for her but she had ulterior motives that I was too young to see through. But Massimo was right and I learned from it.'

Massimo was right? So he'd stopped whatever unfortunate affair Emiliano had gotten involved in?

'I'm focused on nothing but racing now.' He smiled

at her good-naturedly. 'Massimo is very protective, but very soft on the inside. He stays in the office so his anxiety doesn't infect me. But you know this.' He lifted his glass towards her. 'Life is full of risk and uncertainty, but it must be lived.'

Emiliano was only a few years younger than her, but he had an innocent candour about him.

'Those are awfully wise words for a nineteen-year-old.' She couldn't resist lightly mocking him.

'They're my sports psychologist's words.' He sent her an oversize conspiratorial wink. '*He's* ancient.'

She laughed and he laughed, too. Open and honest, he lacked the brooding intensity of his cousin. In fact, he was surprisingly balanced for a highly ambitious athlete.

'Truly, he is wise,' Emiliano added. 'Massimo got him for me.'

Of course Massimo had. That was what Massimo did. He sat at his triple screen setup and fixed everything from a distance. Got in all the experts anyone could ever want. But surely, Massimo had never thought Lily was any threat to Emiliano in Singapore. By then he *well* knew how serious she was about her job. It didn't make sense.

'It's evident you adore each other.' Emiliano smiled over her shoulder. 'He can't take his eyes off you other than to frown at me now.'

Lily barely breathed. If Emiliano saw it, everyone would see it. Her love. His *lust*. And as mortifying as that was, she suddenly had the sinking feeling worse was to come.

'When did that clip of us chatting go up?' She tried to keep her tone light, but her throat tightened.

'Oh, it was weeks ago now.' Emiliano shrugged.

Not Singapore, then.

'Don't worry.' He reassured her. 'They swamped it with my latest Hearnshawe clothing campaign.'

Of course *they* had. Massimo would have used the PR team and taken care of every last little detail.

She suddenly remembered the conversation. It was the only time she'd talked to Emiliano beyond a polite hello. In Canada, weeks ago, about tyres again. Only hours before she'd flown back on the cargo plane and met a sexy *stranger* on the plane.

Only he'd not been a stranger, had he? Massimo had planted himself there deliberately. Because—as he'd acknowledged—he would do whatever necessary to protect Emiliano. To protect Hearnshawe. But wow, hadn't it blown up in his face this time? Now he'd had to do even more to protect his heritage.

She'd been a *strategy*. Entirely. He'd never been interested in just *her*. She couldn't even delude herself that irresistible sexual chemistry had drawn them together and fate had thrown a curveball. He was an *actor*. She'd been a passion-starved pushover. He must think her pathetic.

And the worst of it was, it had almost worked.

Tonight she'd been revealed as Massimo's lover and so it would be normal for Emiliano to laugh and talk with her. Of course they would be friendly. But Massimo had overplayed his hand. Emiliano himself had let the cat out of the bag. The whole thing had been a setup. She'd been nothing but a chess piece. He'd thought so little of her, didn't even see her as an actual *person*, just a threat.

'That's a great campaign.' Lily's mouth gummed up. 'I loved the long-sleeved tee.'

'Massimo will get you one, won't you, Massimo?'

'Won't I what?' His low voice was right behind her.

She turned, rocking back on her heels at the brilliance in his astute blue gaze. The wave of betrayal was overwhelming. She'd never felt as unwanted in her life. She didn't take the drink he offered her. She couldn't fake it, not even in front of all these people.

'Are you okay?'

Of course Massimo noticed. He was so damned observant, seeing everything and ready to swoop in and save the day. But it wasn't heartfelt concern for her; she was merely another of his many *details* to take care of.

'No.' She eyeballed him. 'We need to leave. Now.'

CHAPTER ELEVEN

THE DRIVE BACK to the hotel was very different to their earlier journey. Sure, he put up the privacy screen, but there were no teasing whispers. No intense *closeness* or dazed desire. It was all a con. Lily couldn't trust herself to speak, so she counted, trying to blank out the shame pouring through her. He'd used her so badly.

He said nothing but he was too intelligent not to know there was an issue. Which meant he had the self-control to wait for complete privacy for an argument, but no concerns about seducing her in the very same semipublic space. Which told her everything she needed to know—sex with her meant nothing to him. It was just a convenient add-on to this situation.

'What happened?' he asked the second they were inside their luxurious villa. 'Did someone say something? Was it Emiliano? You know he's very young.'

'And yet, he's not as emotionally incompetent as you.'

She marched into the room. He didn't. He remained near the door, immobile aside from the muscle twitching in his jaw.

'You didn't need to worry about him,' she said. 'You didn't need to defile yourself to defend him from me.'

'Lily—'

'You are so full of shit,' she snarled. 'Insisting our different backgrounds don't matter?'

'They don't.'

'Yet, you were so worried I was some threat to Emiliano, that you made the oh-so-noble sacrifice of sleeping with me so then I'd be your sloppy seconds. Did you think your young cousin would have too much loyalty to you to be interested? Newsflash, Massimo, he was *never* interested in me and I was never interested in him.'

'I know that.'

'*Now*. But you didn't then. That night on the cargo plane, you asked about my job in P1 to see if I'd spill company secrets. You wanted to know if I fancied the damned drivers. You were pathetic.'

He huffed out a heavy breath. 'It wasn't like that.'

'No? Then why were you even on the plane when you have your own jet?'

His gaze dropped, avoiding her eyes. Guilt. Discomfort. It didn't matter.

'You boarded deliberately because you knew I was on it, didn't you? You knew my name.'

At the deep point where all the pain welled, anger now erupted. She'd thought that *issue* as he'd called it, the chemistry between them, had been the one area in which they were truly *equal*. The only arena in which they met on the same level. But even that had been a lie.

'You think so little of him, but he never once said anything inappropriate to me. Never once flirted. Never once moved too close. We talk about tyre compound. That's all he and I have ever talked about.' She whirled away, unable to stand looking at him she was so hurt.

'You think even less of *me*.' Anger curled within her.

'Did you honestly think I'd fall into bed with either of you? With *anyone*? You really saw me as a weapon that had to be neutralised?' She couldn't believe it. 'I was lonely that night and I'm not going to apologise for thinking I'd met a fellow free spirit and indulging in a moment. But you, *sir...*' She whirled and spat the words at him. 'You have so much to grovel about. You didn't just conceal your identity, but your *motives*. If I'd known who you really were, I never would've gone near you.'

'Which is why I didn't tell you!' He exploded. 'And I know that was wrong. I know there are no excuses, but I lost my head. I sat next to you for ten seconds and—'

'No. *Don't.*' She wouldn't hear false declarations now. 'It really blew up in your face, didn't it?'

'How things began is irrelevant. Don't let a minor detail wreck the progress we've made.'

It was hardly a *minor* detail. 'You think progress can be built on a pack of lies?'

'I know I screwed up. I can only try to do better. But I am responsible for—'

'You're not—'

'We're *both* responsible for this baby,' he growled. 'We both have to do what's best—'

'But we don't agree on what is best and we never will. Because *I* am not like you.'

Because unlike him, she wasn't *only* concerned about the baby. She had feelings for *him* as well.

'Doesn't anything I've done since then count?' he argued. 'Don't let your damned need for independence blind you to the bigger picture. I've respected your wishes as best I can, Lily. I can support your work and study. I've taken care of your family. I will never abandon you the way they did. I will never abandon our child. You can trust—'

'How have you taken care of my family?' she interrupted. 'What about my family?'

He snapped his mouth shut.

'What else haven't you told me?'

He drew in a deliberately deep breath. 'I was going to tell you. I was just waiting until…'

'I was fully under your spell?' she finished for him sadly. 'What have you done?'

He lifted his chin. 'I've purchased your parents' business.'

'You what?'

'They were happy with the deal.'

He'd made them a *deal*. Had he done that while she was doing press-ups by the pool? 'And that's important, you think?'

'I think it'll help.'

Of all the things he'd stunned her with tonight, she would never have expected him to be naive.

'Until they burn through whatever money you've given them and then come back for more,' she said bitterly. 'So they get the payout you promised I would never see.'

'Lily—'

'Don't kid yourself that you did this for me. They could have threatened your reputation but apparently, you've bought their obedience. You really will do anything for Hearnshawe.'

'The garage still exists. There's a new accountant in place. They just wanted to get above the breadline.'

'So you know them better than I do? Despite having never met them personally?'

He looked tense. 'They just needed some help.'

'Oh? Is that all? I'm amazed he told you that. That he let you do all that. You out-alphaed the alpha. You want applause?'

'Well, I'm not sorry I did it,' he said defiantly. 'When Finn gets out of jail, we can get him work at the factory. Reintegrate him.'

She gaped, appalled.

'What's your next trick, resurrecting Callum from the dead?' She was so hurt by his interference. 'They don't even talk to me and you've…' She gasped for air. 'You've *rewarded* them.'

'You were worried they would be a problem. Now they won't be. I fixed it.'

'How gangster of you. Are you pleased you have everything perfectly within your control now?' She blinked furiously. 'Doesn't it matter to you how they treated me?'

'What matters to me is that they don't hurt you *more*. They're not going to bother you.'

They would *always* bother her. She was hurt that he didn't see that and he hadn't talked to her before doing anything.

'So you just sorted it all behind my back like some delightful surprise? Like you sorted the problem of Emiliano talking to a mechanic you can't trust?' She couldn't believe him. 'You're not a fairy godmother with a wand to fix everything. Don't you understand that some things can't ever be fixed!'

'Of course I know that!' he roared. 'But this could be made better.'

Not better. *Unbearable*.

'We can work together, Lily.'

'Well, this wasn't us working together, was it? This was you doing whatever was necessary to get full control. Of me. Of them.' Just as he had his damned company. 'Is Emiliano never to be allowed a girlfriend while he's racing?' she asked.

He blinked. 'What?'

'Because you don't want him to have any distractions. Focus is all-important. Right?'

He shoved his fists into his pockets. 'It takes time to learn to compartmentalise.'

'Do you think you compartmentalise?' she scoffed. 'You have no balance at all. It is nothing but work. You have no real family relationship with him. You have no social life. Barely a sex life and heaven forbid a love life. You've cut everything *but* work out of your life. It's unfair to ask Emiliano to do the same. Don't project your own failings on him. As I said, he's not as emotionally incompetent as you.'

'My failings?'

She stared at him and slowly shook her head. 'The thing is you *almost* had me. You almost got everything you wanted—my stupid surrender. Do you know I actually was starting to really *like* you?'

More than like. And he knew it. Because he winced.

'We don't have much in common at all, Massimo. I might be independent, but *I'm* not heartless.' She swept her hair back from her face. 'In the car tonight when you couldn't resist me, I felt so desired. I thought I was truly wanted.'

She'd thought he ached for her in the way she ached for him. That what was between them was something whole and lovely and *more* than anything she'd known before.

'You were wanted. You *are*.'

'No, I'm only ever a means to an end.' She pressed her fist to her chest. 'I needed to be eliminated from Emiliano's radar. But then I got pregnant so I had to be kept… *satisfied*.'

She'd been such an idiot. She'd wanted to achieve; whether anyone noticed or not, she just wanted to move forward in her own life. And now it felt as if he'd taken all of it away from her. But he'd also given her something she would always protect.

'Lily, don't—'

'Call it as it is?' She could hardly stand to look at him. 'You're a hypocrite. So noble in your quest to get Hearnshawe to succeed, upgrade safety mechanisms, protect Emiliano. But it's all a smokescreen. You're just ruthless. You did just want revenge on your grandfather. You blur the lines to get what you want, which makes you as morally grey as my family. In fact, you're even more self-centred than they are. You're like the man who hurt you most. You're him, needing to keep an iron grip of control over everything in your life.'

As controlling as his grandfather. As her father.

He whitened. 'I don't just make unilateral decisions. I build a team, defer to expertise. I do my best—'

'I'm not talking about the team or even Emiliano now. I'm talking about the rest of *your* life. The massive amount that you just ignore. I thought it was arrogance, but actually it's just sad.'

Anger flickered in his eyes, but he didn't respond. The truth was he never would have given her a second glance.

'You never wanted to marry. You never wanted me. You never wanted this baby. So let's just say it's not yours,' she said. 'Then you can just go away and stay away.'

'I can't do that.'

'Yes, you can. You have to. Not for me, but for yourself. I don't think you even know what you truly want.' She dropped her gaze. 'You've spent all your adult life trying so hard to take care of the company, take care of Emiliano. Everything to honour your parents because you think you failed them. You think you failed me, too, except that did take *both* of us.'

Silence.

'But I won't be another thing you have to feel guilty about and do your best with. Your entire life you've been working to someone else's blueprint. You should have better favourite things to do than choosing from colour swatches on a screen. Are you brave enough to go for what *you* actually want?'

Did he know what that even was? Couldn't it be her? Why couldn't he want more from *her*?

But he didn't answer.

'You're not sacrificing the rest of your life for me,' she said huskily.

'You're going back to a caravan in the bottom of a garden over my dead body.'

She braced. That harsh whisper told her so much. She didn't give a damn about the luxurious lifestyle he could offer. She'd live beneath a bridge if it meant she could truly be with him. *He* was what she wanted—and for him to truly want *her*.

But he didn't. He just wanted to ensure she was okay and that wasn't enough.

'You don't want me to suffer in any way because of

the baby, right?' Tears filled her eyes. He cared, but not *enough*. 'I won't suffer because of the *baby*. I'm going to leave Singapore on the next available flight,' she said shakily. 'Don't try to wear me down, it won't work. I will live wherever you want as long as it's *apart* from you. You can see the baby if you really want, but you don't come near me, because *that* is what will cause me to suffer. Don't *you* come near *me*.'

He didn't. He didn't move. As far as she could tell he didn't even breathe for a solid two minutes. And she was spent—silenced by her own stupid emotion.

'Okay,' he finally spoke. 'I'll make the arrangements. You and the child can be free of me, from Hearnshawe, too, if you think that's best.'

That wasn't what she thought was best at all. That wasn't what she wanted him to say. But he'd not fought. Not tried to convince her. He capitulated, completely.

And she was devastated.

CHAPTER TWELVE

MASSIMO SET UP his workstation. Angrily. Dictated messages. Scanned documents. Studied the spreadsheets. Angrily. Only he was *happy* to be alone, back into normal routine. He would *not* remember her quietly turning her back and boarding his jet. Alone.

Her stoicism infuriated him. She'd taken *nothing* else into consideration. She'd been so extreme—allowing one detail to destroy everything. They could have worked out. They could have found an arrangement that would be perfectly acceptable. Instead, she'd overreacted about his real reason for boarding that cargo plane. It had been a spontaneous impulse to ensure she wasn't a threat to his cousin, and that had been more about Emiliano than her, and within two seconds of boarding she'd been a total threat to *him*.

He abandoned work and made arrangements for her instead—seeing he couldn't shake her from his mind he might as well get all the ideas into action. He sent a deluge of tasks to his assistant in England. Then he glanced out the window, but Berlin couldn't hold his attention. He rolled his shoulders and turned back to his screens. He damned well just needed to get on with it. Work was always the answer.

Lily had reckoned he kept ridiculously busy. But the periwinkle debate was the frivolous tip of an endless, urgent to-do list. He'd always been determined to eliminate distraction because when moving at speed distraction was dangerous, but now he wondered if *work* itself was the distraction. The perfect tool to avoid everything else. Because to his horror *nothing* on his list now seemed to matter all that much. And now that he had nothing to fill his head anymore, he was left alone with…

Fucking *feelings*.

He paced away from the screens, circling the room. He'd had a completely *tolerable* life until she'd shown up and thrown her damned spanner in his works. She'd made him spin like an out-of-control car hitting one barrier after another.

He did everything fast, all the time to avoid stopping. Because when he stopped, the feelings caught up to him and the feelings weren't stopping now. Everything uncomfortable and emotional *slammed* into him. He tried to breathe through the spate of memory fragments and facts he'd not allowed himself to consider in forever. Feelings he never, ever wanted to dwell on. Loss. Loneliness. Desolation. Guilt. All so damned inconsolable.

Lily had looked unconsolable three days ago when she'd implied that any suffering she might feel was because of him. But if she really felt anything serious for him, how could she end *everything* so easily? Because she'd been looking for a reason to and he'd been looking for a reason to let her. He'd taken the push and turned it into a shove. He'd let her flee, not fought to stop her, because when she'd directly asked what he wanted, he'd *frozen*. His inability to answer had been answer in itself.

He'd stepped back the second he could and she wouldn't ask again because she'd been hurt before.

Lily was the only woman who'd not just kept up with him, but moved even faster than he did. She'd beaten him in several ways. She'd certainly beaten him to understanding his own damned deficiencies. She'd questioned what he really wanted—just for himself. He couldn't answer because he couldn't ever consider that he could have what he really wanted. Now he made himself face why.

He wasn't worthy of having what he wanted. How could he take happiness when he'd wrecked so much in the past?

He was unforgivable. He couldn't *ever* get his parents' forgiveness. Nor could he forgive himself for what had happened that day. He couldn't ever make it *right*. Intolerable shame burned through him. But now it was worse because he'd let Lily down, too. Lily, who was carrying his baby.

He'd lost so much and been left with so little, because he'd not let anyone else in. Nor had she. They'd both worked to prove themselves. But where he *deserved* his lonely hell, *she* didn't. She should have what she wanted. The problem was she *wanted* him.

He gnawed the inside of his cheek, hating the dilemma. If he was what she wanted, then maybe he needed to make himself worthy of her. Only he didn't know how. Because she was everything he wanted and he wanted her so much it terrified him.

Suddenly, he was so sick of himself. Hell, he was actually so needy. So much for being strong; he was problematic as hell. *He* needed fixing. That was more important than anything else on his damned list.

NATALIE ANDERSON   185

He'd been navigating everything alone for a long time. She was right; he'd done a great job in the professional aspect of his life, but he'd avoided the personal entirely.

He could bury himself in work all over again—like he'd done for more than a decade—or he could sit with the horrible ache of regret—feeling isolated and deprived—and try to forgive himself.

He lasted about five minutes before he realised that sitting and doing nothing wasn't going to work, either. He needed to take *action*. He just had to work out what. But maybe he didn't have to do this alone at all.

He flew to Budapest for the next P1 race. He made himself go into the garage, barely withstood the death stare Shane shot him nor the pointed coolness from all the other mechanics. Great. As it was, he was trying not to feel her absence as a physical pain. She should have been able to keep working for a while yet but he'd wrecked that for her. He went in search of his cousin. He'd not wanted Emiliano to face the Hearnshawe pressure alone so he'd put a team in place around him, yet he'd kept a *personal* distance and he shouldn't have.

He found Emiliano studying the track on a computer simulation in his suite. He glanced up, surprised when Massimo slumped into the seat next to him. 'You okay?'

Massimo's facade of complete capability crumbled. 'I don't know what I'm doing.'

'Does anyone?' Emiliano fully turned, then switched the screen off. 'What's wrong?'

Massimo swallowed but the tightness in his throat didn't ease. 'Lily's gone.'

'Yeah, Shane isn't happy.'

'She's pregnant.'

'Oh.' Emiliano's eyes widened. 'Congratulations.'

'I don't know what to do.' He didn't want to admit that he'd let her go. That he'd let her down.

Emiliano fiddled with a tag on his racing suit. 'Is it all that complicated?'

Yeah, it sure as hell was. 'She thinks I only want to marry her because of the baby.'

Emiliano's eyebrows shot up. 'And is that true? Because if it's not, then you need to tell her whatever the actual truth is.'

'It's not that easy.'

'Because you're afraid you won't get the reaction you want?' Emiliano pulled a face. 'Talk to her so you don't have to live with the eternal regret of not trying.'

Eternal regret? Massimo shook his head. Yeah, he had enough regret already. The terrible mistakes he'd made would always haunt him. He couldn't make more. Which meant doing more—doing *better*. Because Lily was worthy, he had to try—and *keep* trying.

'When did you get so smart?' he grumbled. 'You've only just turned nineteen.'

Emiliano puffed his chest playfully. 'My psychologist is a genius.'

'Yeah? I'm glad.'

'Seriously, I have a really good team around me, thanks to you.' Emiliano reached out and patted his shoulder. 'I know you got this, bro.'

Bro? Massimo chuckled, but at the same time was suddenly overcome. He'd arranged Emiliano's team but thought he was on the periphery of it. He *should* be closer to his cousin. He wanted his own personal team, too—with Lily as his co-pilot.

He rubbed his chest. He was so tired of being without her. 'Would you mind very much if I miss this race? I think I need to go home.'

'I don't mind as long as you bring Lily to the next. I'd like her tyre expertise.'

Massimo almost smiled. 'I'll see what I can do.'

Emiliano was right; *honesty* was at the heart of it. Lily wouldn't live a lie. She had integrity far beyond most people. She'd withstood enormous pressure from those closest to her—her family—and resisted. She was true to herself and she needed honesty from others if she were to let them close. No wonder she'd been furious with him for not being honest about who he was on the plane. But he'd done worse to her by not being honest about how he felt. He didn't want to marry her because of the baby. Not for reputation or security or any other reason other than the plain fact that he wanted *her* in the very centre of his life. Whether she could forgive him, whether she still wanted him, didn't matter. The very least she deserved was the truth.

CHAPTER THIRTEEN

LILY GRITTED HER teeth as yet another delivery van pulled up in front of the cottage. What on earth could it be now? She couldn't think of a single thing she needed, but the man thought of every tiny unnecessary detail.

She'd been here almost a week, living in the gorgeous cottage Massimo's assistant had brought her to when he'd picked her up from the private flight she'd endured all alone from Singapore. She'd wanted to hate it but she couldn't. Tucked behind an enormous brick wall with wrought iron gates, with its two bedrooms and cosy living room, the picturesque country cottage was just a half hour drive from Hearnshawe HQ. It was no enormous soulless mansion in which she'd feel lost, but annoyingly was the perfect size for *her*. Though the grounds were big. The pretty front garden was filled with flowers while at the rear, there was a double garage, plus another large shed. Apparently, a small resistance swimming pool was being installed in there next week. Boxes of gym gear and crates of mechanics tools had been arriving all week. A builder had also appeared to ask endless questions about her setup preferences for both her workout and workshop spaces. Two days ago a gleaming car had been delivered—the one she'd told Massimo was her favourite in the Hearnshawe range, fresh off the factory floor in cornflower blue. It had to be a custom paint job. She'd tried not to look at it but lasted less than ten minutes before running her hand over the sleek design, then sitting inside and breathing in the beautiful interior fit. Massimo Hearnshawe created nothing but the absolute best. That was what he was doing for her now, too—setting her up with everything she could ever possibly need. She had to let him. This was the agreement she'd insisted upon. She would stay where he wanted, as long as *he* stayed away from her.

She took the parcel from the delivery driver with a weary smile and set it on the dining table with the three others that had arrived yesterday. She was too heartsore to open them and too reluctant to dare contact Massimo and tell him to stop it. She couldn't risk any direct contact.

Instead, she turned back to the large screen in the lounge that had been installed on her second day. She couldn't miss watching the next race. P1 Global had made it to Budapest—to a purpose-built track, high speed with lots of overtaking opportunities. Hopefully, Conrad and Emiliano would shine, but she also weakly wondered if she'd glimpse Massimo in the background. It was unlikely; he was too adept at avoiding cameras and controversy since toppling his grandfather those few years ago. Too *calculating* to be caught.

It was great he would do anything for his cousin. That he would do everything to protect his unborn child, too—even insist on marrying her. All his actions were rooted in protectiveness and a deeply held sense of duty. Obligation and responsibility was all he allowed into his life. There was no real fun or laughter or love. He stared at colour on a screen instead of *experiencing* it. He guarded his heart with deliberately impenetrable walls because he felt guilty.

His grandfather had hurt him so much he'd literally locked him out of his life. He'd locked Lily out, too, but that wasn't because she'd hurt him—he'd never actually cared enough to be hurt. He'd just been annoyed because she wouldn't agree. So he'd worked around her regardless with his high-handed, fix-it-all mentality that devastated her. In all their time together he'd had an ulterior motive to protect someone else. She'd never been his first consideration. She'd not been that for her parents, either. Their rejection had been bad enough, but Massimo's actions stabbed even deeper. He'd slipped beneath her barriers so easily. He'd made her laugh, he'd made her relax, even made her begin to *trust* that they were connecting on more than that physical level. But it hadn't even been that. She could never get past knowing that he'd only been on that cargo plane to test her. He'd never actually wanted just *her* in any of the intimate moments they'd shared.

Then she'd been stupid enough to ask for that most vital part of him anyway—unable to stop herself from *hoping* that maybe there had been more for him in the way there was so much more to it for her. He'd frozen. He'd not argued. Not fought for her. He'd just let her go. Silently. So easily. Because she was *not* what he wanted and never really had been.

But being broken-hearted didn't mean she was incapable. She would study, rebuild her career, eventually repay him for the cost. She'd started over completely before; she could do it again. Better this time—better for her baby.

A knock on the door interrupted her ruminating. Another freaking delivery so soon? Muttering beneath her breath, Lily stomped out to answer it. 'Yes?'

His eyebrows arched.

Her jaw dropped.

In the resulting stillness she absorbed his drawn features, the tired-but-wired intensity in his tall stance, the perfectly cut navy shirt that fitted his lean frame and deepened his blue eyes. *This* was the reason she'd needed a complete break from him. Because it only took *one* look and she was utterly weak already. She would resist. She folded her arms across her chest.

'I—' He broke off and cleared his throat as the unmistakable soundtrack of the P1 opening credits blared from behind her. 'You're watching the race?'

She hesitated. Nodded. 'Did you want to—'

'Yes.' He moved forward.

She pressed back against the wall so he wouldn't brush against her, then closed the door. She wasn't going to remember what happened the last time they'd watched a race together. She was going to be *strong*. But her delightful cottage suddenly felt far too small.

'I've been getting a lot of deliveries,' she muttered as she followed him into the lounge. 'Most of them aren't necessary, Massimo.'

His lips twisted into the smallest strained smile. 'I brought you this.'

He set an envelope on the little table near her.

Paperwork? She definitely didn't want paperwork—not a cheque or some contract that would put her further in his debt. 'What is it?'

'The results of the paternity test, I think.'

'Is that why you're here?' Lily pressed her hands together, trying to shrink into herself.

'No.' He couldn't seem to take his eyes off her. 'I've been an idiot. I screwed up, Lily. I'm so sorry.'

Lily didn't want to ask what he was sorry for. Honestly, she was afraid to breathe in case he flitted away and she'd be left alone again. That this visit was actually just a figment of her wishful imagination.

'I should have told you why I was on the cargo plane,' he said. 'I should have talked to you about your parents before doing anything for them. There are so many things I should have done differently. I moved too fast and I'm sorry for rushing you. But I can slow down. I can explain.' He didn't slow, though, he paced, unintentionally emphasising the snug dimensions of the space. 'A lot of people are drawn to Hearnshawe. There's history, past success. People want a piece of it. Several targeted Emiliano. They're more wary of me.'

'Maybe it's that cold reputation you've cultivated,' she muttered. 'I get it, you're wary about new people in his life.'

He stopped in the middle of the room, his blue gaze fixed on her. 'I watched those four seconds of him talking to you and all I saw was a pretty neck and delicate jaw and a hint of honey-coloured hair. I wanted to see the rest of you. I got the barest glimpse on the plane before it went dark. Then we talked and then I just wanted you all to myself. *Not* being Massimo Hearnshawe for a few moments, flirting with a fascinating woman who was funny and bright—I was spellbound. That impulse overrode everything rational in me.'

Lily stiffened. She'd been an *impulse*.

'When we landed you recognised me on the tarmac and you were furious. You didn't want anything to do with *me*. It was humbling. And yeah, it was bad enough that I was effectively your boss and if I'd said anything more then you'd have quit and I didn't want that. I tried to step back. Tried to respect your wishes. I kept my distance. But I watched you and the more I watched, the more I learned and the more I liked. Then I thought we could have a party in Singapore, that I could see you outside of work. Which I know is stupid because it was a work party, but I was desperate and I thought I might get to see you in a dress. But then you were late. And then...' His shoulders lifted. 'I was so rude to you when we first found out, but it wasn't long before I realised I wasn't angry. I was scared. But I wanted it, because I wanted you.'

Lily was having a hard time processing everything. She stepped back, sinking her weak body onto the sofa. 'Are you saying you came to the Singapore race just to see me?'

'Everything I've done in the last two months has been with *you* as the primary object in my mind.'

The whole two months? 'You came to more races.'

'Yes.'

'You arranged a party just to see me in a dress.'

'Yes.'

'You were ridiculously nice to my parents.'

'I wasn't that nice to them.' He looked rueful. 'I own their garage. I own their home. I told them any contact was up to you, and only if they apologised. I also told them if they upset you in any way, if they harassed you, then I'd change the locks and throw them out on the street like they'd once done to you.'

'Oh.' A wave of emotion buffeted her. 'You're right. That wasn't that nice,' she whispered.

'No.' He stared at her unwaveringly. 'I'm sorry. I never should have done any of that without talking to you. It won't happen again.'

She shook her head slightly and spotted the envelope. 'Don't you want to open those results?'

'The result doesn't matter to me.' He thrust his hand through his hair. 'I want you. You and everything that's yours. I will love your baby. I will deal with your family however you want me to. Because at the end of the day, it's you I want.'

Lily looked down. She couldn't handle this. She couldn't believe—

He suddenly dropped to his knees right before her. 'I hate living without you beside me. I miss your laugh. Your bite. Your brain. I wanted you from the moment I saw your picture. I liked you from the second you spoke to me in that dark cargo plane. Honestly, I think I fell in love with you instantly. But I didn't think I could have you, Lily. I let you leave. I let you think I didn't love you.'

Emotion clogged her throat, so she choked. 'And that's not true?'

He slowly shook his head. 'Our baby is infinitely precious to me, because it's part of you. I will love and adore it the way I love and adore you.'

Tears scalded her eyes, blurring her sight. 'Why didn't you say so sooner? Why didn't you *say*?'

His hands gripped hers. 'I failed my parents, Lily. I wrecked their lives. How could I have all this happiness when my actions deprived them of the same? How dare

I claim everything they lost? Everything I don't deserve? How dare I be that damned selfish?'

She flinched, hating his pain. His hold on her tightened.

'But then, how dare I not?' he said huskily. 'I can't go back in time. I can't ever earn the forgiveness I want from them. But I *can* spend my future being better for you—loving you, loving our child. Putting you first. Because how dare I deprive *you* of all that you deserve?' His hands shook as he held hers. '*You* deserve all the things, Lily. You deserve the world. And if by some miracle you do still want *me*, then I am yours.'

'I don't want the world or all the things,' she said raggedly. 'I don't want anything but you.'

'I don't deserve you, but I can't deny you.' His smile was agonised.

'You do deserve me,' she muttered fiercely. You do.'

He pulled her to her feet and kissed her. Reverently. *Fervently.*

'I missed you,' she sobbed.

'I'm here now and I'm never going anywhere without you again.' He gripped her waist in that wonderfully strong, familiar way.

Lily leapt, finally believing. She wrapped her arms and legs around him. How she'd yearned to wind like a vine around him like this again. Burying her tear-streaked face in the side of his neck, she clung tight. She'd missed how safe his size made her feel. When she felt the soft sheets beneath her, she knew he'd found her bedroom but she kept her eyes closed. Like that first time, there was only touch and sound and heat and it was everything.

'I love you, Lily.'

She heard his smile, felt his wonder. All-consuming tenderness enshrouded the passion that had always flared so swiftly between them.

He brushed his cheek against her burningly delicate skin. 'I missed you so much.'

'Yes.' Broken apart, she trembled so much she could barely move, only able to surrender to him completely. *'Please—'*

'I told you I can slow down.'

'I don't want you to slow down,' she half-laughed, half-wailed. 'I want you to love me.'

'I do. Will. Always.' He punctuated the promises with kisses. 'Always. Always. Always.'

He moved so deliberately, deliciously slowly—kissing her, caressing where she was most sensitive. But it was the infinite care with which he did it that had her shaking and incoherent. When she was pure putty in his arms he finally pressed home. Her breath quickened as a riot of need overwhelmed her. Absolute emotion—*all* of the emotions—suddenly stormed through her in a cacophony of blazing intensity. She couldn't contain her cries. His words tumbled, too—hot and incoherent. There was no slow anymore. There was only passion. Only *love*.

A long time later, she heard the race commentator roar the results on the telly.

'Oh no.' Biting her lip she softly chuckled. 'You're missing another Emiliano podium.'

Massimo ran his fingertip across her belly in a possessive swirl. 'He was okay with me missing the race as long as I bring you to the next. And all the rest.'

'You talked to him about me?' She quivered but not from the tickling sensation.

'Annoying creature seems to have it all together—talent and brains. Told me to get my act together.'

He rose onto his elbows and she saw the uncontained happiness in his eyes.

'I want to spend the rest of my life at your side, Lily. I want to have this baby and others if you do. You can design a race car and I'll build it, but only *if*—' he paused theatrically '—you let me choose the livery.'

'You want final say on the colour scheme?' Joyous laughter bubbled up and burst free. 'Is that the deal?'

'Yeah, that's the deal.' He wrapped around her, imprisoning her in the best ever embrace. 'I want it all with you, Lily. But I promise I will never ask you to marry me again.'

She snuck a breath. 'You won't?'

His tender, teasing smile widened. 'I will marry you anytime, anywhere, anyplace. When *you're* ready, just say the word.'

'What word?' she muttered, rendered brainless by his touch.

Laughing, he pressed even closer. 'You'll work it out.'

CHAPTER FOURTEEN

Five months later

LILY WOKE WITH a start, seized by the sudden conviction that she'd made an outrageous mistake. She'd been an absolute *idiot*.

'Massimo?' Rubbing her stiff back, she hurried down the long carpeted corridor.

It was a very long corridor. She'd moved out of the cottage only days after he'd come back to her and into this, his large estate only ten minutes from Hearnshawe HQ. It turned out the cottage was on the farthest end of the enormous property. She had to admit she'd gotten used to his stellar living standards shamefully quickly. In the early months they'd travelled in his jet to all the P1 races, resting at his other properties in between—the lakeside villa in Italy, the apartments in Paris, Venice, Barcelona— until she'd become too pregnant to fly. She'd been thrilled when Hearnshawe claimed second in the car construction category—even more thrilled to see Massimo celebrate with them. In the driver's rankings, Conrad had placed second and Emiliano fourth. Lily felt certain Hearnshawe would climb to dominate both categories next year. For all Massimo's pleasure in the team's ascension, he was still a competitive beast who wanted to win.

'Massimo?'

She found him in their study where he had a triple screen setup permanently in place. Her computer and notebooks were at the other end of the long table. She'd aced the bridging course for her university prerequisite and would start her first engineering paper next semester. Just the one so she could spend time with him and the baby, too. Some days she went to the factory just to hang out with Shane and the other mechanics, keeping her hand in. But now she felt panicked—contentment had blinded her.

Massimo glanced up and immediately rose. 'What's—'

'Will you marry me?' she interrupted him breathlessly.

He gaped, then crossed the enormous room in three strides. 'Lily—'

'I love you. I want you to be my husband. I want everything official, for our baby to—'

'Yes.' He swept his arms about her and pulled her close.

'Can we do it today?'

'What?' His laughter rumbled, a heavenly sound that she was too stressed to appreciate. 'Why the sudden rush?'

'Because I love you and I've been an idiot for—' She winced.

'What's wrong?' He stiffened.

'Twinge in my back. I must've slept funny.'

He smoothed his strong hands down her spine, drawing her to lean against him completely. She flexed beneath his ministrations, his touch soothing the panic and setting desire alight instead.

'So can we?' she mumbled. 'I don't care where or how—'

'Do you know I have a spreadsheet of all the possible options?' Laughter still threaded his voice, but there was an undercurrent of the deepest sincerity. 'It's my favourite thing to dream about—whether we're by the lake in Italy, or on a beach in the Pacific, or the ballroom here at home. Whether we have caramel or chocolate cake, whether we invite the entire company or just a few, and most of all whether I have a periwinkle or cornflower-blue tie with the ribbon around your bouquet matching—'

'Cornflower. Always. Matches your eyes.' She nudged his chest. 'All those options sound amazing. Which do you prefer?'

'Any,' he answered simply. 'All that matters to me is that we spend the rest of our lives together and that's going to happen whether we marry or not.'

'But I want us to marry. I...' She closed her eyes as he gently kissed her.

'We will,' he promised.

She heard his utter determination and knew it would be done. When he decided on something, he delivered. And always for her. Now her anticipation flared as he pushed the robe from her shoulders and turned her so he could press feather-soft kisses across her back. His hands kept up the deliciously firm strokes, caressing ever more intimately until Lily circled her hips with increasing impatience, any last anxiety evaporating in the blistering heat.

'Have I told you how much pregnancy suits you?' He shaped her curves—warming, teasing, loving.

'Every day,' she murmured, utterly distracted by the flickering tease of his hands.

'And you're so ready for me.' He nipped her skin approvingly and she heard the slide of his zip. 'Zero to a hundred in seconds.'

She pushed back, taking him as deep as she could, almost passing out in the profound pleasure of being with him. 'Oh *yes*.'

'So fast. So perfect.'

They lost words, but gained grip. Sealed together, they moved in exquisite friction until they hit that finish line together.

'Come on, shower.' He scooped her up. 'Then I'll show you my big spreadsheet over breakfast.'

Chuckling, she let him carry her to the bathroom. 'I've been such a fool.'

'No, you haven't.' He ran the water and tested the temperature. 'Nothing wrong with needing time to trust.'

'I do trust you,' she said. 'Completely.'

He smiled. Vulnerability softened his edges, revealing the deep emotion he'd always hidden before. Lily kissed him then stepped under the warm spray while Massimo stepped back to strip.

'Oh,' she suddenly gasped. *'Ohhh.'*

'Are you starting round two without me?' Massimo teased.

'No—*oohhh*!' She gasped and clasped her stomach. Her backache was worse but her whole middle had tightened and—'Oh, I think my waters have broken.'

'Seriously?' He lit up and immediately yanked his pants back on. 'I'll grab the bag, call the helicopter. We'll be at the hospital in no time.'

'But I'd wanted us to be married before—'

'Our baby is in a hurry, darling.' He wrapped her in an

enormous towel and kissed her nose. 'Which shouldn't be a surprise knowing us, right?'

'But it's *too* early, isn't it?'

Massimo held her shoulders firmly, his gaze calm and assuring. 'It'll be okay. Trust me.'

'Yes. But we should have—oh!' That vise tightened around her again.

Massimo could move incredibly fast. In less than an hour they were in the private hospital suite, but Lily was stuck on her regrets.

'I should have—' She winced.

'Hold tight.' Massimo held out his hands to her. 'I'm not going anywhere.'

Three hours after their arrival at the hospital, Lily showered, immeasurably grateful to the nurses who helped her into the lovely silk nightgown that Massimo had produced from the seemingly bottomless bag he'd packed. When she settled back in the freshly made bed, Massimo had vanished. Their son was swaddled in the bassinet beside her. He'd arrived two hours ago, a little early but in perfect health and he was endlessly, utterly fascinating.

'Where have you been?' she murmured accusingly when Massimo walked back in a few minutes later.

'Why aren't you resting?' he countered equally accusingly, but his severity lost all impact as he produced a beautiful bouquet of flowers from behind his back.

She shot him a wide smile. 'I can't stop looking at the most beautiful baby in the world. He's so tiny.'

'I know. He's our treasure.' Still holding the flowers, Massimo sat on the edge of her bed and gazed first at their baby, then at her. 'Do you still want to marry me or was that labour pain talking?'

His voice was uneven and he looked a little wild about the eyes.

Lily leaned in. 'I wish we'd married *months* ago.'

'Well, there's no reason why we can't get married now.'

'Now?' Her heart clattered. 'Is this one of your impulses?'

'One of the better ones, yes.' He chuckled. 'There's a chapel in the hospital. There's a chaplain. A few people are coming to meet our little boy, but they'll also be brilliant witnesses if you'd like. Do you think he'll mind sharing his birthday with our wedding anniversary?'

'You're serious.' Lily's aching body hummed and she stared at the flowers he held. At the cornflower-blue ribbon tying them together. The blue that matched his eyes. 'Is that my wedding bouquet?'

He reached out and caressed her cheek. 'We can have a big party later—affirm the vows with a proper suit and a pretty dress but you couldn't look more beautiful than you do right now, Lily. What do you say?'

'Yes.' It would *always* be yes.

They wrote their vows in a laughing rush of ecstasy. Emiliano arrived to be best man and with immense thoughtfulness, Massimo arranged for Derek and Jean to support her. Intimate and special, it was the sweetest celebration. And as Massimo slid a heavy gold band on her finger, her heart had never been so full.

After champagne and cake and cooing, Emiliano, Derek and Jean finally left. Lily sank back into the bed and watched her handsome, enchanting husband cradle their tiny boy.

'Not much of a wedding night for you,' she whispered sleepily.

'We had a wedding *morning* to remember forever,' he teased. 'And I couldn't be happier than to spend the night watching over our son while you finally get the rest you need.'

She *was* awfully tired. 'I love you so much,' she mumbled.

'And I love you.' His answering smile was so tender it brought tears to her eyes. 'You've given me everything, Lily. Absolutely *everything*.'

She didn't want to slip into sleep. The sight of him with their baby was too sweet, and to live with love like this was too wonderful.

'Come on, sleepyhead.' Massimo flicked the lamp by her bedside off and whispered a loving little tease in the darkness. 'It's lights out and away we go.'

Yes. Bathed in the security of his love, she finally realised that this was only the *start*.

* * * * *

Did you fall head over heels for
Boss's Mile-High Baby? *Then why not explore*
these other sizzling stories by Natalie Anderson!

Billion-Dollar Dating Game
Their Altar Arrangement
Boss's Baby Acquisition
Greek Vows Revisited
Enemies Until After Hours

Available now!

Get up to 4 Free Books!

We'll send you 2 free books from each series you try
PLUS a free Mystery Gift.

FREE
Value Over
$25

Both the **Harlequin Presents** and **Harlequin Medical Romance** series
feature exciting stories of passion and drama.